Out of Evil

ELEANOR RILEY

Out of Evil

Trilogy Christian Publishers

A Wholly Owned Subsidiary of Trinity Broadcasting Network

2442 Michelle Drive, Tustin, CA 92780

For information, address Trilogy Christian Publishing

Rights Department, 2442 Michelle Drive, Tustin, Ca 92780.

Trilogy Christian Publishing/ TBN and colophon are trademarks of Trinity Broadcasting Network.

For information about special discounts for bulk purchases, please contact Trilogy Christian Publishing.

10 9 8 7 6 5 4 3 2 1

Library of Congress Cataloging-in-Publication Data is available.

ISBN 979-8-89041-560-8

ISBN 979-8-89041-561-5 (ebook)

DEDICATION

To my family:
Elizabeth, Esther, my grandson Matthew,
and my loving husband, Cecil.

"May we always find green pastures and still waters,
as it is said still waters run deep,
and the depth of love will
keep us rooted and grounded in God."

Acknowledgments

I recognize that without God, I would be a complete failure. Therefore, I thank Him for releasing His imaginative workstation within to bring out this novel, *Out of Evil*.

Special appreciation to Dr. Veronica Lyle, educator, for her contribution in editing *Out of Evil*. I am aware it is a tedious task, but you have worked assiduously to complete this project. Thanks so much.

I'm expressing much appreciation to my children, Elizabeth and Esther, for their ideas and thoughts and also their unwavering support, as always.

I would like to thank the editorial staff of Trilogy Christian Publishing for a job well done.

TABLE OF CONTENTS

PREFACE

You are about to walk into an intriguing world of what can happen to anyone who has determined to allow God to be the center of their lives and who will permit themselves to make the best out of what life has to offer. None of us should settle for less. Let's not get into the habit as so many others do. Don't be envious of anyone's legacy. Keep trusting God, and our reward will be superior to anything we can ever imagine. If we do His will as He commands us, the blessings He has for us will be like the sands on the seashore.

The responsibility is ours to accomplish not only for ourselves but also for our children's children. Life's pathway may be a winding and treacherous one, but the many encounters do not matter. If God leads us, we will find our way.

> *"If you don't know where you are going,*
> *you'll end up someplace else."*

> Yogi Berra

To every dreamer: keep hope alive. There are novels in all of us. It's time to get busy. Put your imagination to work, let it run wild, and it's guaranteed that you won't end up someplace else.

INTRODUCTION

Rose Alexander was a strong-willed young girl who grew up in a large community but lived a sheltered life. One thing outstanding about her was she was passionate for clean relationships and good, moral Christian living with a high regard for decency and a passionate love for God, marriage, and family. She found true love from a stranger on a rainy spring night in Boca Raton, Florida.

Rose's life was always yearning for that faceless rationale she could not pinpoint, but she knew that something exciting was in her future. Haunted by the death of her parents, which she imprecisely remembered by photographs and ghostly blurred images only, she came to understand and cannot forget how their lives were unexpectedly brought to an end in that horrifying plane crash when she was only four years old. Rose Alexander decided to make a change of environment, seeking belongingness and overcoming the ghost of the past.

This is an exciting novel about a young girl moving from uncertainty, loneliness, and forethought of an unfortunate life designed for failure to a life of fulfillment, love, and happiness. God turned things around for Rose Alexander, who once stood on the brink of projection of lifelong hard work and unsuccessful ventures; she was now brought to what the Bible spoke of as "that blessing that will overtake us by the way" (Deuteronomy 28:2).

Rose met Peter Swazi on a rainy and stormy night in Boca Raton. Swazi, looking forward to spending his usual long weekend with his mother, ran headlong into disappointment, devastation, and death and manifestly was now expecting loneliness and a life that his mother lived—reclusion. Rose Alexander fell in love with the man of her dreams and was determined to make it better, in spite of the many interferences and a near-death experience.

God bears our desires, our needs, and our aspirations in His hands until He sees that we are ready. It does not matter which epoch or persuasion. True love will work in any marriage with the determination to make God the head of it.

Rose had the desire to walk down the long aisle of Saint Paul's Cathedral someday. This refuge helped Rose elevate her hopes and objectives. This was where she found attention-grabbing evidence of the love of God embellished in every decor. Yes, here, at last, the day came. Peter Swazi waited for his bride, Rose Alexander, at that old-fashioned altar as the organ played "Here Comes the Bride."

Chapter 1

Winter was just on the verge of ending, and one could actually smell the air of spring wafting around. It was a day when the thermostat seemed to read at least ninety degrees. Mostly everyone was hanging out, some doing quick errands, others sitting at curbside restaurants and having quick lunches, while some spent their time just appreciating the warmth.

Rose opened the gate from her aunt's house in SoHo and mused, *I'll go for a walk. I think I deserve a few minutes of interaction with God to distinguish which direction He wants me to go and what my next move will be.*

Taking advantage of the amazing weather, Rose found herself sitting alone by a fountain in Downtown Manhattan, lost in thought about all the effort she had exerted in making sure her scholastic work throughout her life had paid full dividends up to then. She was satisfied that, finally, she was a graduate of Pace University with a degree in banking and finance and also had a bachelor's degree in theology obtained from the School of Theological Seminary of California, along with other distinctive accomplishments.

Young, gifted, and black,
We must begin to tell our young,
"There's a world waiting for you.
Yours is the quest that's just begun."

Nina Simone[1]

This was the song that she used to pump her ego whenever she felt unachieved. *I am twenty-two years old*, she told herself. *College and university are all behind me. This sheltered life has me wedged like a recurring decimal. Emailing job applications and having interviews perpetually, I feel wasted, and the worst part is that I am not able to secure a position.*

Between these perplexities, Rose had thought to sign up for driving lessons. If she learned how to drive, this would broaden her scope and the possibility of acquiring a job. Taking public transport had become tiresome, especially during the summer months, when everyone had the desire to go on vacations and do other outdoor activities, especially outside the city. She was happy when she completed the lessons, took the driving test, and passed for a New York State driver's license. *There's a world waiting for me out there. I need to be able to exhibit my God-given accomplishments and abilities without restrictions.*

Rose decided to change her environment and move to a state she knew nothing about, but with God's guidance, she knew she would find success and happiness. That afternoon, upon returning from her walk and enjoying her communication with God and connection to self, she knew it was time to have that particular conversation with Aunt Stella.

The argument between them veered off in the exact opposite direction she expected from her aunt, Stella, which gave her a stronger desire to move on. "Rose," Aunt Stella began, "I took full custody of

---

1   Nina Simone, "Young, Gifted and Black," on *Black Gold*, 1970.

you after the death of Mark and Mary. You were only four years old, and I cared for you like my own daughter. I do believe I have done the very best above and beyond, making sure you were never wanting in any aspect of your life. I really don't expect you to reside here forever, but thinking of moving to another state is entirely illogical."

"Why do you think it's preposterous, Aunt Stella? What's so wrong with me desiring a life of my own as opposed to living one that's suitable for you? Furthermore, I am twenty-two years old, Aunt Stella. Don't you think it's time that I finally fly out of your nest? A bird my age would have died a long time ago from old age. I am sorry I cannot be that bird. I refuse to stay here until I am old and gray. I need a chance to see what it's like to be on my own."

"Well, Rose, if that's the way you look at it, then have it your way," Aunt Stella said condescendingly, made herself a cup of tea, and went to bed.

The next morning, Rose began her search for a new house in which she wished to move as soon as possible. The money she had, she was sure it would be enough to swing the deal. *I know this will be a fresh experience, but God told me He will never leave me or forsake me. Therefore, I am standing on His promises.*

Included in Rose's habit of reading the daily newspaper that morning was the purchase of several other newspapers and the weekly gazette; she came across an advertisement in the House for Sale section. "The cute Tudor-style house nestled in a secluded enclave is reasonably priced, located at 2 Saint Paul's Place, Boca Raton, with the magnetic attraction of the beautiful and ancient Saint Paul's Cathedral." She was excited to see the words *reasonably priced.* She called the realtors immediately and set up an appointment with them. They had offices in New York, so there was no need to fly to Boca, which was a blessing.

She had the necessary requirements when she met with the realtors and was accepted without hesitation. She was promised that, as soon as the appraisal and inquiries were completed, she would be given an appointment for the closing. They added that the house was newly built by contractors who came to Florida to experiment with a new type of roofing that would enable occupants to enjoy the sound of torrential rain showers that would formulate the echo of raindrops like musical entertainment without being alarmed. The hurricane season would soon arrive, so this was a good time to observe and experience the state-of-the-art roof experiment.

After a short while, Rose's prayer was answered, and she realized her dream. She received the keys to her new house and soon had her furniture shipped from New York. She was now beaming with pride and great expectations, which gave her a good feeling of accomplishment and propriety. She was 100 percent sure she was heading in the right direction. Moving from the hustle and bustle of New York City to Boca Raton debuted her feeling of independence and excitement. An earth-shattering change was what Rose yearned for.

A few weeks after Rose's move to Boca Raton, she decided to familiarize herself with the community and immediate environment. She began taking short walks in the mornings and afternoons, introducing herself to her new neighbors and finding the convenience stores and the like. One afternoon, as she closed the door to her beautiful brick and wood-framed house and set out on her usual trek, Rose observed that there was an ominously cloudy sky and mused that there was no mention of a storm brewing on the local weather forecast. Inclement weather patterns are a staple in Florida, so she was sure that she had time to do her walk and explore the majestic Saint Paul's Cathedral mentioned in the advertisement when she purchased the house, even though for the past week storm preparedness was emphasized. She was excited about visiting Saint Paul's. It was always open for visitors to go in and pray, which was just a stone's throw from her house.

The sound of a grass cutter could be heard from the houses situated on the quiet street of Saint Paul's Place. The landscapers were making sure they had done their job before the rain began. Saint Paul's Place was named after the ancient Saint Paul's Cathedral, built in 1932 during the war and with the presidential election of Franklin D. Roosevelt. That was the church where everyone would assemble on any given day for worship, sightseeing, or whatever the occasion may be. Hearts would also yearn to employ their great occasions there, especially weddings, tea parties, bingo nights, and, of course, funerals.

The grounds of the cathedral were graciously designed, and the lawn well manicured, with tall palm and pine trees outlining the landscape and periphery of the magnificent garden. Passersby gasped at the beauty of this historic cathedral. They were intrigued by the beautiful magnolias and hydrangeas boasting a picturesque hedge that surrounded the cathedral.

Inside, the furnishings were original, ornate, and unique; the carvings, moldings, and stained glass images made by artists and carpenters long before the eras of modern furnishings were pristine and reverential. There were plants deliciously arranged in front of the podium as though a royal celebration was imminent. A fresh, sweet fragrance filled the atmosphere from the various floral arrangements, giving the ambiance of peace and contentment. A mixture of different types of roses, tulips, and running garlands was the scene of a botanical fixture.

The organ was brightly polished; the drums and other musical instruments were spanking clean as if they had never been played. The choir pews were upholstered in red and accentuated with gold and a touch of blue. The water jug and glasses were sparkling as the evening's setting sun shone through the giant stained glass windows, illuminating them. A picture depicted a lost sheep, with the hand of Jesus, the Redeemer, outstretched, motioning for the sheep to come.

This magnificent painting could be seen from any angle; everything about the sanctuary was strategic and beautifully arranged. The serenity of the presence of the Supreme Being could be felt, which sent a divine connection as if to say, *Yes, God is here.*

Rose's thoughts spiraled almost uncontrollably down the winding path of her many dreams and aspirations as she lost her being and desires in the grandeur of the cathedral and became oblivious of time. The sharp sound of the pipe organ suddenly jolted her out of her reverie, and she realized that she had lost consciousness of time. It was getting late, so she scampered off to her regular evening walk. It was dusk by then, but she still determined due diligence and kept pace with the regular bikers down the path that had become famous for after-hours business workers doing their routine exercises.

There were a few students sitting on benches and beneath old oak trees with study materials as Rose nonchalantly walked the usual path as she mused that this rainy period was unusual; it came much earlier, ahead of the seasonal hurricane months. Toward the end of March, the torrential showers of April had been the breaking news and continued for quite some time. The meteorologist had issued hurricane preparedness and that there would be intervals of heavy rains. From her experience and from old sayings, had she taken an umbrella, it would not rain. Trying to prove that the old sayings were right, Rose ignored the possibility that it would rain before she returned and intentionally left home without a plan of defense against possible bad weather.

All along the path, one could see flowers in full bloom, scoping the entire area. The roses were almost saying "*ciao*" as Rose made her way through the side of the path that was beautifully gardened with a variation of summer foliage. As she walked, her imagination took over. Alone in a new environment, trying to gather ideas and psychologically making plans for her future, she became engulfed in all sorts of possibilities, envisioning the beautiful Saint Paul's

Cathedral and walking down the aisle. She made a mental vow to offer her services there, with her bonus of a degree in theology.

The incessant thoughts of her parents, who were killed in a plane crash when she was only four years old, now flooded her consciousness. *If I had them*, she said to herself, *I am sure life would be somewhat different than it is now.* She also remembered her only aunt, who cared for her after the death of her parents, and a handful of friends and classmates left behind in New York. As she walked, she rehashed the plane crash, which she read from the old newspapers she received from her mother's neighbor, Mrs. Fields, who lived only doors apart at 16 Greenwich Avenue in SoHo. Rose frequently envisioned the photographs of her parents that were published at the time of the crash and wished it never happened.

The *New York Times* headlines read, "Wall Street Executives and Hedge Fund Couple Mark and Mary Alexander Died in Horrific German Airlines Plane Crash." She bore an almost identical resemblance to her mother. She thought of her aunt, Stella, and how she had never discussed the death of her parents for whatever reasons. Rose respected this unwritten law but secretly wished she could have a heart-to-heart family talk with the only mother she knew—Aunt Stella.

"Anyway, this is good for me," Rose said out loud. "My parents would be proud of me, trying to stand on my feet." To be independent, mature, and levelheaded was a blessing. She considered herself lucky to have gotten this far in life as an orphan. She thanked God as she went along.

Rose's mind was now a swirling, surmounting conundrum, but in all of her meanderings, she remembered the scripture: "I can do all things through Christ which strengthened me" (Philippians 4:13, NKJV).

Rose walked, unaware of her surroundings, without realizing how far she had gone. "Well, let me turn around now," she whispered. At that precise moment, she felt raindrops and knew she was going to be soaked by the time she made it back home. Rose hastened her steps, looking hurried and panicky with an odd feeling of being followed. This distracted and disturbed her.

"You can come under my umbrella." The voice from behind startled her. "I am sorry. I can see that you did not hear my footsteps."

Rose knew he was right; she was deep in thought. "No, I did not hear your footsteps. However, for some reason, I had a sinister feeling of being followed."

"Here, come under. You are drenched," the stranger said.

She had no choice but to take cover under his umbrella. "Thank you so much. I forgot to take my umbrella." She knew she hadn't but purposely left it as she thought it would not rain before she got home.

"My name is Peter, Peter Swazi. What's yours?"

"Oh, Rose Alexander, I was just doing my evening walk, got carried away, and have gone far beyond my normal distance."

"I understand," Peter responded. "Sometimes I get carried away with so much, especially if I have a lot on my mind and by the beauty of my surroundings. How far a distance is your house, if I may ask?"

"About forty-five minutes," Rose responded.

"Goodness! You would be as wet as the road by the time you get home without an umbrella," Peter said.

The lightning that accompanied the rain was more than frightening. One bolt of it sent Rose involuntarily clinging to the arm of the stranger she met just a few minutes before. Her trembling hands crept up involuntarily and clutched his neck tightly; he could barely catch his breath. "Oh my goodness!" Peter exclaimed. "Are you okay?"

With an embarrassing smile, Rose assured him she was and tried unsuccessfully to compose herself.

"It's already late, Rose," Peter said, looking at his watch. "My house is only a few yards away from here. It's not safe for you to continue walking in this storm. I will not allow you to risk your safety. Please come with me. I can grab hold of some warm clothes and make you a cup of tea until the storm passes. Mother would be delighted to welcome and make you comfortable."

The wind had gotten really fierce, destroying everything in its path. Some trees were uprooted, and roofs were blown off, swirling around them as though they had found themselves in the middle of an angry tornado. A few cars had stopped offering them a ride, but Peter politely thanked them with the assurance he was only a few blocks from home.

With a few seconds of silence and a look of uncertainty and distrust, Rose hesitantly accepted Peter's offer and followed him home, desperately clinging to him, quickly reassuring herself that the mention of his mother was a comforting thought. Above the howling wind, she yelled, "Sure! I believe that's a good idea! Thanks."

In just a few minutes, they were on Matt Court Road, within feet of Peter's house. Close to the bend, Peter noticed that there was an ambulance along with a sheriff's car parked at what seemed to be the entrance to his house. He immediately hastened his steps, walking away from Rose. Without realizing it, he had unwittingly discarded the umbrella, and the wind instantaneously swept it across the street and into the woods. Rose became frightened; she did not bother going after it for fear she would be blown over by the strong gust of wind.

With a look of sheer panic and long strides, Peter was just in time to watch the paramedics placing his mom onto the gurney and rolling her toward the parked ambulance nearby. His eyes bulged, and his breathing became raspy as he gulped for air. With tears streaming down, he identified himself to the police and the paramedics and asked what happened to his mother and why they were taking her to the hospital. He then began screaming hysterically. One of the neighbors intervened, held his hand, and gave him a quick explanation—that it was an accident due to the storm. One of the trees in the backyard became uprooted and fell on the house, crashing through the bedroom window of his mom while she was asleep, wounding her and knocking her unconscious.

Rose actually saw Peter rush into the ambulance, and his mother was seemingly barely breathing. She stood speechless when a woman approached her.

"Poor girl!" she exclaimed. "Can I help you? You appear to be a stranger to the neighborhood?"

Rose was afraid to volunteer any information as she stood there soaked and trembling.

"Can I get you anything?" she asked.

"No," Rose replied. "I must be on my way. Thanks for your kind gesture."

The ambulance sped off with its screaming siren as Peter sat with his mother's hands in his. Rose could tell by his gesture and posture that Peter was praying earnestly while assuring his mom that she would be fine without knowing the severity of her injuries and relying totally on his faith. The highway to Boca Raton General Hospital was wet and foggy. The storm continued to rage, but in any event, the ambulance cautiously sped through all the stoplights and signs with sirens and flashing lights, hoping all vehicles would take precautions; of course, they had close calls and near misses but managed to arrive at the emergency entrance safely. Peter was not sure whether his mom had heard him praying, but he was desperately hopeful. Peter had completely forgotten about Rose.

The weather got miserably worse, and Rose was scared to death that a tree might just fall on her or that she would be swept away with all the loose objects airborne. The wind and rain did not let up, and the tall pine and palm trees were visibly bowing and twirling in command of the wind. Reassuringly, Rose observed that the lightning had subsided.

She walked cautiously but was frightened, wet as the road. She tucked the lesson learned in the corner of her mind—never leave home without observing the weather and never ignore warnings. She also made a silent vow to ignore old wives' tales. This time, no one bothered to stop and offer a ride as the few vehicles seen outside were cautiously inching their way to their destination; she was alert, carefully dodging flying objects, praying that she would get home safe and not be injured or harmed.

"Ah! Thank God!" she exclaimed as she opened the front door. The day seemed to be a long one. She undressed while making her way to the bathroom and dropping her clothes piece by piece behind her. The rain had subsided somewhat by the time she got home. A shower was all she needed to revive her. Her house robe felt like a rescuing arm around her as she walked to the kitchen to make herself a cup of tea.

The television was turned on, already on the weather channel. Of course, the forecast was not what she had expected. The storm intensified, and there were storm warnings up to six o'clock the next evening. Everyone was asked to remain inside until they were further advised.

What do I do here all by myself while waiting out the storm? Who do I call? Rose questioned herself. *I can't call my friends in New York. They are quite a distance away, not able to assist anyway. Should I call Aunt Stella? No, I am in no mood to hear her "I told you so."*

Fear gripped her with the realization that she was all alone in the middle of a vicious storm. The sudden ringing of the telephone amplified the fear; it seemed loud and threatening, and she was terrified to pick up the receiver. It was past midnight, and she had no idea who the caller could be."

"Hello. Can I help you?"

"Rose, it's Peter." With a sad voice, he apologized for rushing off, leaving her alone to maneuver her way through the storm, and for not calling her before now.

Before Rose accepted his apology, she first asked, "Peter, how did you get my number?"

"You gave it to me, remember? Yes, you did. I made a mental note and had no problem recalling."

"Oh, I was so overwhelmed with the storm I just totally forgot I did. I have never experienced this type of weather. In New York, we barely have storms, not to this extent, anyway. How is your mother?"

"Mom is critical, Rose. The doctors advised me she may not make it through the night. It's touch and go as far as they are concerned. She was crushed inside with internal injuries beyond their capacity." As Peter spoke, he broke into sobs; it broke Rose's heart to the extent that she decided to join him at the hospital.

"Do you mind me coming out to the hospital, Peter? After all, I can give physical and moral support and, in the meantime, say a prayer."

"No, Rose, say a prayer where you are," Peter replied. "You can get through to God faster than coming here. Everyone has been asked to stay off the roads. The storm isn't finishing anytime soon, and I would hate to know there is more devastation caused by it. All we need is for it to be calm. The meteorologist reported it has intensified and upgraded to a category one hurricane. I also noticed there are others here with injuries from storm-related accidents. I'm so heartbroken, Rose. And to be honest, I could use a shoulder to lean on, but keep praying for her. I will keep you informed."

"Okay, Peter, thanks. What if I need to call you? I don't have a number." But by then, he had hung up and did not hear her question.

Four days went by, and Rose heard nothing from Peter concerning his mother's condition. She thought of visiting the hospital but was not sure which section she was taken to or if her presence would be welcomed. The storm had passed, but there were reports of major and minor injuries to some of Boca Raton's residents, now recovering. There were so many homes that were ravaged and left desolate. The electricity took days to be restored. Everyone was now anxious to see better days.

In Rose's prayer, she thanked God that He showed her favor and kept her electricity on. That was so awesome. Most of her neighbors were without power.

Rose had barely slept since the storm, and the thought of what she had gone through haunted her frequently. She was experiencing anxiety attacks one after the other and began to question her move. She had to consciously use this time to pray and thank God for His protection and guidance. It was only then that she would drift off to a fitful sleep.

It was two o'clock in the morning when the phone rang. "Hello."

"Hi, Rose, it's Peter. Sorry for calling at this time."

"Hi Peter, don't worry about the time. What's the latest? You haven't called. I have been worried sick about you and your mom. How is she?"

There were a few seconds of silence. "My mom passed away two nights ago, Rose."

"I am so sorry, Peter. Can I help with anything?"

"Yes, you can. The funeral will be tomorrow evening at seven, with the interment on Tuesday morning. I would love it if you are able to attend."

"Where will the services be held, Peter?"

"It will be at Saint Paul's Cathedral. I believe that's near you, is it?"

"That's the beautiful church a few blocks from me. I was there a few days ago. I am quite familiar with the location. Yes, of course, I will attend. See you then."

An entourage of cars lined the streets near the church, with most people dressed in purple, black, and gold, unwittingly accentuating the royal decor of the church. There were employees from Peter's job, well-wishers, and, of course, the parishioners. Peter was sitting on the front pew with his head bowed and tears streaming down his cheek. Rose was able to navigate her way and sit next to him as if she were a member of the family.

Without hesitation, Peter clung to her arm as if to say, "I needed you to be here right this minute." That almost took her breath away.

"You will be okay, Peter. The Bible says, 'Precious in his sight is the death of his saints.'"

"Mom is okay." A smile took the tears away, and one could see he was somewhat consoled.

Rose tried looking around, observing everyone. The church was packed to its capacity, with standing room only. *It is obvious that she is remarkably loved*, Rose thought.

"She was an ardent parishioner in good standing," Peter said with a smile as if he'd read Rose's thoughts. "For forty-five years, she has been here. Yes, she served well. This is her second home. She volunteered here almost every day. I was born, baptized, and raised in this church. My mother was an only child like I am. She was never married."

A questioning expression danced across Rose's face fleetingly. Luckily, Peter was distracted by well-wishers giving their condolences. Rose was hoping he would not return to the subject, but he did; he picked up right where he had left off, as though he could not wait for the attendees to leave him for a minute.

"Well, Mother lived a partially recluse life," Peter continued. "She was an orphan, and up to the time of her death, she would always talk to me about not having the privilege of growing up with her real parents. Her real parents had died when she was eight years old during the war, and the records at the registrar only showed her adoptive parents, Mr. and Mrs. Joseph Swazi. They were Germans, and at the time of adoption, Mary's name was changed from Mary Spencer to Mary Swazi. She remembered her parents' names were Matthew and Diane Spencer."

"This entire story she would repeat almost every time I was with her for a long weekend. I do believe the idea of being adopted stayed with her all her life, but because her parents were already dead and she was properly cared for, she assimilated into the lifestyle of her new family and made many adjustments when they relocated to the United States. Mom said that there was no known address in Germany for the Swazis, and to be honest, I had no interest at all in researching it. Maybe if I had perused the family tree, I would locate my family, but that's no good for me now. It does not matter anymore." Peter rambled on as if he was trying not to focus on the immediate event.

Rose quietly sat and listened to him as he narrated his mom's life story. "I'm so sorry about your mom," Rose replied under her breath. "I just wished all this had not happened. I am here for you now. You are going to be just fine. I can somewhat identify with where you are now, but the worst thing with me is I only vaguely remembered my parents through photographs and newspaper clippings. God kept me and provided for me through my aunt. She saw to it I was taken care of. I am confident that He will take care of you just the same."

The funeral service began; Father Hurling, the pastor of Saint Paul's Cathedral, led the ecclesiastic body as he read from his minister's handbook, "'I am the resurrection and the life.'"[2]

Usually, the family would remain seated. It was only then that Rose was seriously convinced that Peter was her only family, and he chose to stand. He was now beet red as the tears welled up, but he resisted his expression of grief, fearing his associates may think he was weak.

Rose looked in her purse for a tissue in case he needed it but had none. Just then, one of the dutiful ushers handed her a beautifully decorated napkin box. She popped out a few tissues and squeezed them into his hand. She noticed that he did not bother to use them as he thought he had it under control.

Unanticipatedly, in a split second, Peter was out of control. Rose guessed that he realized his mom had been taken from him

---

2   "Jesus said to her, 'I am the resurrection and the life. The one who believes in me will live, even though they die;" (John 11:25, NIV).

so suddenly and without warning, and he lost it. At this point, there was nothing anyone could do to calm him down; he was just overwhelmed with grief.

Someone motioned for Rose to take him outside for fresh air, but she felt resistance when she tried to. Peter refused to part with his mother's casket. He held on to Rose's hand so tightly; she got the feeling that, at that precise moment, he realized that all he had was the girl he met a few days ago in the storm. With a reassuring squeeze of his hand, she whispered, "It's okay. We will be there for each other."

Rose was a bit bothered despite the fact that it was a large gathering; the parishioners, well-wishers, friends, and neighbors had such good comments about Ms. Swazi, yet there was still an unfilled, deep, impressive sensation that there was something left unsaid. At the end of the service, Peter was greeted by almost everyone, saying final words of commiseration and offering help if ever he needed it.

At the end of the service, everyone was reminded of the interment the next morning at ten o'clock. It was just a short service with a final viewing on Tuesday morning. Everyone gathered half an hour for that before interment.

Father Hurling spoke for fifteen minutes, thanking everyone for their support at this time. He also addressed Peter with words of comfort and gave short counsel on how to deal with such a terrible loss. He then led the procession to the far corner of the church grounds for burial. This personal touch of not being buried in a public cemetery was reserved for notable members in good standing at Saint Paul's.

They all walked across to the grave site, where Father Hurling did the committal and gave the benediction. Afterward, short words of condolences were given near the grave site, and everyone greeted one another with words of strength and comfort, but special efforts were made to greet Peter with offers of help if ever needed. Father Hurling took from his pocket an envelope and handed it to Peter, who shoved it in his inside jacket pocket, expressing thanks nonchalantly as if he was expecting it.

The sky gave them just enough time for the committal before the rain came. They all hurriedly made their way back to the church for shelter and a quick repast, where words of comfort continued. "Rose," whispered a voice from behind. She looked around, and she was in awe to see one of her long-standing friends from New York, Abigail Suarez.

"Hello, Abigail. What are you doing here? Are you vacationing, or have you moved here too?"

"My husband and I have been here for two years already, Rose. It's such a divine place to reside. It's beautiful, and the neighbors are very friendly and helpful."

"Gosh, it's so good to see you. How are you?"

"I'm fine, Rose. How are you doing, and what are you doing here?" Abigail asked.

"Well, I live ten minutes away."

"When did you leave New York?" Abigail asked.

"A few months ago," Rose replied. "I needed a change. I just had to relocate. New York was suffocating after I graduated from college. I did not imagine it would be so difficult to find a job. I've done quite a bit of interviews, and the results were always the same: overqualified or getting no results at all. I told my aunt, Stella, whom I love to death, that I had decided to relocate as New York just wasn't working in my favor."

"Abigail, you know that I am a creature of habit, so it took me a long time. I was agonizing over this decision. I prayed, and I questioned God about His plan for my life— you know how it is—and one doesn't make a move as serious as this without talking it over with the Lord and asking Him for guidance. He gave me the green light, and here I am.

"Abigail, I prayed to God for the plans I believe He has for me. I was much too sheltered to perform it," Rose said with a shy smile. "Don't worry, Abigail, you know I was very much involved in the Shrine Church of Saint Anthony while in New York. At this point, I would never forfeit my service to God. I am now seeking information on Saint Paul's policy on how to volunteer for service.

"I am also waiting on God's guidance to situate me in the area of greatest need, knowing that He may not come when we need Him, but He is always on time. I am here now—a new life, a new beginning. I don't know what else is in the mind of God for me, but wherever He leads, I am ready to follow."

How time flies! It was two years already since Abigail moved away from New York after her marriage to the well-known Wall Street banker Todd Baker of the New York Federal Reserve Bank. He had requested to be transferred to the Paradise Bank branch in Boca Raton as his parents were advancing in age and needed him to be near. He was also their only son.

Peter stood a few feet away, talking with one of his neighbors. Engrossed in conversation, he had not noticed Abigail and Rose's interaction. "Come, Abigail. Meet my friend Peter, whom I recently met under tragic circumstances. It's his mom who passed away. You might know him since you were present at the funeral. Do you know him?"

"Hi, Peter, so sorry for your loss. To answer your question, Rose, no, I don't know him," Abigail responded. "But I know your mom, Peter, from a distance and sometimes exchanged waves with her while in her backyard. She was a quiet neighbor, to be honest. I live behind her house. I'm on Deer Court Drive. And we also sometimes glimpse at each other by the produce market, but that's all.

"I knew she had a son. We've just never had the opportunity to meet. My work schedule never allowed me to even ring her bell. She seemed to be quiet and busy. From what I've observed, she frequently goes to church. And before you know it, she is back in the house."

"Is that so?" Peter exclaimed. "How long since you've moved there? May I ask?"

"It's only two years since my husband and I came to live on Deer Court Drive. We just never saw you. I've always wanted to meet her son, though, whom we have heard so much about. It seems he was never home." Abigail looked questioningly at Peter.

"I am home on a few weekends," Peter responded. "My job keeps me away most of the time."

"What do you do?" Abigail asked.

"I am an airline pilot. I do numerous flights each week, so I am hardly ever home."

This was the first time Rose was hearing what Peter did for a living. She never asked, and he never volunteered. As a matter of fact, everything was in such a whirlwind that he never got around to telling, and she never got around to asking. And maybe from Rose's report of her parents being killed in a plane crash, he steered away from that conversation.

There was an awkward, short silence after Peter spoke. Rose dug in her purse to get some leftover tissue. Her eyes welled up with tears at the remembrance of her parents and the plane crash. Whenever this happened, she was a little embarrassed because she often told herself that she was over the effects of missing them. She was very young, but as time went by, she realized conversations on airplanes sent uncomfortable signals of the memory of them, thinking that things would have been so different if they were around.

Abigail chose this brief period of awkward silence to extricate herself with the excuse that her husband was waiting at the bend in the car. "Bye, Rose," she said with a big hug, and then they exchanged phone numbers. "We will be in touch." Abigail had not noticed that Rose's countenance had saddened when she walked away.

"My goodness, what did Abigail say to you that caused such a dark countenance?" Peter asked as Rose tried to camouflage the tears.

"It's not that serious, really. I just had a flashback when Abigail asked your occupation, and you told her you were an airline pilot. Spontaneously, my mind went back to the old newspapers I've read so many times, and I was a little overwhelmed."

"You know, Rose, maybe you should not keep those old newspapers around anymore. The incident was too tragic for you to keep reminiscing, and it was eighteen years ago. Try to let it go. I am not trying to disrespect your emotions or cherished memories, but it's time you lay them to rest.

"My mom, I just laid to rest one hour ago. I am still at the church, still receiving condolences from everyone. Her death was also tragic. I will miss her for a long time, and I do feel empty, but for some reason, Rose, having you here, I am comforted, and I know my losing her will remain with me for a long time. She has been such a good mother. I will never ever forget her. Life goes on. Let's focus on the positive, okay?"

"Thank you, Peter. I needed that."

That was the right time for Peter to invite Rose to join him for dinner. "I'd like that very much," Rose replied.

"Okay, my cab is still here. You obviously will be home ahead of me. I'll pick you up at seven, and we will have dinner at the Hilton Garden Inn on Congress Avenue. Do you mind having dinner there?"

"No, not at all. I am not familiar with the area, but I know you are, and I am confident of your choice." Rose started walking home, feeling differently. Although Peter was still in mourning, he was strong enough to provide comforting words to Rose, who seemed so fragile and emotional remembering her parents. "I'll see you in a few minutes." She waved.

Peter watched her walking through the rearview mirror of his cab until she turned the corner. With a sigh, he wiped his face and again gave the driver his address. "Pretty girl!" the cabdriver exclaimed. "I can tell she is not from around here. There aren't many African Americans in this neighborhood."

"Nope, she is a New Yorker, born and bred. She has moved here desiring a change in environment and to make a fresh start."

They had a short conversation, but no sooner than the car pulled up at Peter's house had the cabdriver assumed a more serious tone. "Take care of her," he said. "She really seemed to be of a different class."

"Thank you," Peter said curtly. The cabdriver's words reverberated in his consciousness, and with a furrowed brow, he walked quickly up the drive to the stately, imposing structure of his house.

As Peter entered the beautifully furnished house he shared with his mother, he experienced a weird feeling of emptiness. He looked around at all her photographs and paraphernalia; there were quite a few of them. Pictures in unusual-looking frames were placed on two entrance tables and in corners of the living room. Some black-and-white pictures were mounted on walls, which one could visibly see. They had been hanging and situated there for quite some time.

Peter looked around for a long time, missing her, and then went to the bathroom to freshen up. He took his jacket off, and the envelope Father Hurling gave him after the burial fell out. Quickly, he picked it up and sat on the beautiful antique vanity stool his mother had picked up on one of the few trips she had made to her favorite antique store in Miami. With the envelope in his hand, somehow, he hesitated to open it. Nevertheless, he mustered up the courage to see what the contents were.

He noticed there were two folded documents enclosed; one was a personal letter from his mother. The other was her will. She had given them to Father Hurling to be held in the church's safe, appointing the pastor as the executor and cautioning him that it should not be given to Peter until her demise. Peter thought of not reading any of them until after dinner when he was home and relaxed, but he was really curious to see what this was all about. He finally decided to do a quick read to set his mind at ease. He decided on the letter first, reading aloud.

Chapter 2

December 1, 1948

Dear Peter,

If you are reading this letter, regrettably, it means I have made my transition to be with Jesus, and I wish you all the best. You are my only living relative, my child, my son. You are a part of me that I have always cherished.

When you were born, I had no idea how you would be cared for. There were times when all hope seemed lost. I held you close when you were sick unto death with pneumonia. I prayed the prayer of healing and restoration when the doctors shook their heads and walked away. The nights were the worst when your fever soared to 106°, and your tiny body almost succumbed to the enemy called death, but God stepped in on time and healed you.

You have made me proud, and I am grateful for the way you've allowed God to be the axis on which your life spins. I knew I was adopted, and the thought of giving you up for adoption during some hard struggles crossed my mind numerous times. I'd gone to the Agency of Child Concern and submitted my request for you to be released to the next foster couple on the waiting list, but when it came time for me to sign the final paperwork, I changed my mind. I could not feel comfortable with the thought of you going the way I did, even though I was cared for in every way. Therefore, I continued to bear the shame, the rejection, the segregation, and the resentment.

I was friendless, forsaken, and hopeless because of what happened to me, which was absolutely no fault of mine. You have grown to be a fine gentleman, sober and God fearing, thank God. Thanks for being a doting son to me and dedicated to your education in the many schools, colleges, and universities you were blessed to attend. Where you went wrong, you accepted the responsibility and made the necessary corrections to move on. You have excelled, you have achieved, and you are accomplished."

I was acutely aware that you were curious about the identity of your father; however, I am thankful that you have not pressed the issue. I was always frightened that you would eventually gather up the courage sooner rather than later to broach the subject. I do believe my eternal rest will be more gratifying between us as I disclose this secret I've kept for over thirty years. It was among God, your dad, and me. Your performance and your life of decency have earned my eternal respect and gratitude.

I was brought to Boca Raton by my adoptive parents, Mr. and Mrs. Joseph Swazi, where I grew up and finished my education and did well. I attended Saint Paul's Cathedral as my adoptive parents had become members there. I had no knowledge of the love of God, nor was I even introduced to salvation. I thought it was just the right thing to attend church and that that would be good enough. One observation I made was that there weren't any differences between the parishioners' lifestyles in and outside the church. This haunted my consciousness through adolescence. I had a conviction in the citadel of my conscience that there had to be something more. This void caused me to seek more fulfillment.

One day, there was a revival at Saint Paul's. The sermon was convincing to my core. An invitation was offered to those who would like to begin a fresh start in surrendering their lives to Jesus and constructing new things. I made the decision to turn over a new leaf and accept salvation by surrendering my defeated life to God.

By this time, a flood of tears was rolling down Peter's cheeks. He was almost hysterical, but he kept on reading, oblivious of time and space.

I became active with church duties, loving the Lord, and enjoying my newfound life. The Sunday school class became my favorite; it was very informative, as well as Bible studies. The insatiable desire for all things God consumed me.

It's amazing how one could get caught up with the work of the church, and nothing else seemed to matter once you know you are on the right conduit. I am the happiest bird on the limb now, knowing that underneath was His everlasting arm. I am feeling really secure now.

I was fourteen years old when my adoptive father, Joseph, betrayed my trust, and the worst part of it—the guilt behind the deception—was the belief that I was responsible. Late nights, when all should be asleep or if the house was empty, he would act as though he was protective of me. He was the only man I ever trusted; as far as I was concerned, he would never tarnish my innocence in any way or tolerate any harm directed at me. I trusted him implicitly; after all, he is my father.

His advance and grooming were subtle, conniving, and deliberate, with the appearance of doting parental care. He was strong and callous, mean and selfish in his intentions, and before I knew it, I was drawn into his immoral web of deception and abuse. This was a bitter capsule to swallow, but I had no alternative. I was young, naive, and frightened.

He continued this rampage of self-enjoyment for quite some time. I could not divulge this to any other, not even my closest classmates or anyone for that matter. The shame and guilt of the situation engulfed me.

A few months later, I realized there was something strange happening in my body. My whole world collapsed around me. I was having a baby.

I was doing well in school. I was a role model, a junior head girl who was really mature and poised at fifteen, appearing older than I really was. Boca Raton Community High School held me in lofty regard. But I was carrying a secret that could never be disclosed. I could not afford to run the risk of appearing loose and vulgar. Furthermore, I would possibly *become an outcast. I thought of other alternatives but had neither the wherewithal nor the courage—in a word, scared.*

Well, Peter, here you are, my only son, whom I love dearly.

The more Peter continued to read his mother's letter to him, the more he wept. His shirt was now soaked with both sweat and tears. His mother's life had ended tragically without saying goodbye. This day was the saddest day he had ever experienced, and here he was, alone, determined to see what the end was.

He continued reading and hurried to the conclusion, realizing that he only had a few minutes before the promised time to pick up Rose for dinner.

I am glad he's deceased now. My adoptive parents succumbed to cancer a few years ago, he first and then my mother.

Finally, what I had endured to keep us safe is now an old ghost of my past. My shame has ended. It's a ghost I will not see again, no, not here, not ever. You are the pride and joy of my life, and I am so overjoyed that I did not seek to destroy you.

I gave this envelope to Father Hurling, asking that it be conveyed to you in the event of my death or if I should become incapacitated or seriously hurt.

Be good to yourself, Peter. I have left you enough to sustain you. The will explains your inheritance. Allow Psalm 16:5–11 to be your guide.

The letter ended with the date and time she had written it. He realized it was just a few months before she was tragically killed. "This, indeed, was a premonition of what was to come," Peter muttered to himself.

Be careful.
Love always,
Mom

In his captivating interest in the letter, Peter forgot he hadn't read the will but quickly put both letters in his pocket as he rushed out to await the taxi, which was two minutes away. In a few minutes, Peter arrived in front of Rose's house in a bright orange and black taxi at two minutes past seven. He was sure Rose would be outside.

"Could you please tap the horn, sir, so she would be aware we are outside? Thanks." With that, Peter hopped out, swiftly walked up the drive, and waited at the door. He looked debonair in a red sweater with a blue shirt collar sticking out over the neck. He was also in slim-fit blue jeans. His sockless feet in the comfortable brown brushed-leather loafers his mother bought him a few months ago for his birthday gave him a casual yet distinctive look. He wore them for the first time and in her honor.

Rose quietly closed the door behind her, he stepped aside, and she hurried to the waiting taxi. Peter was already standing by the open cab door and helped her in. "Sorry to be late, Peter. I was scouting through my closet, trying to find something suitable for tonight. I hope you like this dress. It was given to me by Mrs. Fields. I discovered she was my mother's closest friend and confidante and also my parents' immediate neighbor from whom I got the old newspapers chronicling their deaths. She gave me quite a number of keepsakes she secured as my aunt, Stella, wanted to donate everything to the Salvation Army. Mrs. Fields hid most of my mother's personal belongings she knew would be sentimental to me when I grew up, and maybe some I would actually label as keepsakes. By the time I got around to using some of the stuff she saved, they were already dated, but who cares? They seemed just right for me," Rose said with a shy grin.

"Don't be silly, Rose. Of course, I like the dress. You look rather amazing."

It was a black linen dress with a lace collar and red trimmings to contrast the red pumps she had bought from Charles David's collection in New York. The dress was made by Giovanni of Paris, which fit her perfectly, and looked as though she picked it out herself.

They both were indulgently occupied in complimenting each other and had forgotten to communicate their destination to the taxi driver. "Oh my!" Peter exclaimed. "Please take us to the Hilton Garden Inn at Congress Avenue downtown."

It was quite a drive to the other side of Congress Avenue, but they made it to the seven-fifty reservation Peter confirmed with the concierge. The pair was escorted to a table for two romantically situated under a red fabric canopy with candlestands holding battery-operated, shimmering lights that cast a soft glow, silhouetting them and making them barely discernible in the dark. The moon was full and ostentatious, and one could count the stars formed in what looked like the Milky Way. It was beautiful and begged to be admired.

The evening was a high-quality one, especially for Peter to enjoy after such a bumpy two weeks of storms, death, and burial. He needed to talk about everything, and Rose impressed him as the person he could feel comfortable with—a soul mate and confidante. They ordered red wine to start, and when the waiter came to take the order, they asked for more wine, which would give them more time to decide on the entrée.

Peter looked a little reserved, and for a brief moment, there was an air of sadness in his demeanor. "So where do you go from here, Peter?" Rose asked to break the monotony and awkwardness of the moment. "Any thoughts on how you plan to go about being on your own completely? Tell me, what do you have in mind right now besides seeing what the contents of the will and testament are all about and the letter you briefly mentioned from your mom?" The questions tumbled out spontaneously.

Peter took a swig of his wine, reached into his pocket for the will, and handed it to Rose. "Please read and then give me all the details. Right now, it all seems a little morbid to me."

As Rose reached for the will, she asked, "How about reading the letter first? I am curious of its contents, Peter."

Peter hesitated, but before he could answer Rose, his cell phone rang and interrupted the conversation. It seemed to be a call of importance. Peter excused himself and took a few steps away for a private conversation. It was about a five-minute conversation, and then he returned to join Rose with a pensive look.

"What's wrong, Peter? Is everything okay?"

"Yes, everything is okay. It's my job. They want me to resume flying as early as tomorrow."

"Oh no," Rose sternly said. "What did you say to them, Peter? You are not in a position to fly just yet. You need more time to recover from the tragic death of your mom." Rose began to really get so upset with the heartless request of Peter's boss that she was brought to tears. "How can they do such a thing to you, Peter?" She felt such empathy that the tears flowed without realizing she was supposed to be strong for him.

Peter knew that he was not ready to return to flying duties so soon but was afraid to request more time off. He was already given two weeks and felt that would be enough time to convalesce. Rose got herself in such a frenzy that Peter had her in his arms, consoling and assuring her that he would be fine. "Tomorrow, I will deal with this, Rose. I will definitely request another two weeks, and hopefully, it will be approved."

In a moment, Rose gathered her composure and was ready to place her order. They both had filet mignon and another serving of red wine. For the next few moments, they ate in silence, occasionally glancing at each other, ostensibly giving time for each to think about what to say next.

As the dinner dishes were being taken away, the realization hit Rose that they both would have to tackle the matter at hand, one that would determine the providential destiny of Peter. Rose asked again about the letter, expressing the desire to do a quick read.

Peter hesitated again and said, "Of course, but I did scan through it quickly before I picked you up. I can tell you some of the crucial contents preferably. Then afterward, feel free to make a comment, as I would like to hear your take on some of the things she said."

"My mother hid the truth about me and who my father was for all her life. She wanted to keep the whole scenario that way as she was not proud of how it happened, and she hadn't many friends she could confide in. She told me from time to time that I was an integral part of her life, giving me the security that nothing and nobody else was necessary in the equation."

At this point, Peter looked like a lost and lonely little boy. Rose clasped her hands over his as he continued, "She didn't think of sharing the load she called 'shame' with me. Had she told me face-to-face, maybe I could have made her burden a little lighter. In a nutshell, Rose, that's what the whole letter is all about."

Peter added in a softer tone, not exhibiting the pain and sadness that was just evident in his narration of the letter, "She wrote some stuff about me, my accomplishments and honesty, and wished me all the best with my future endeavors."

His voice again assumed a whimsical tone. "Sadly, she even mentioned how she wanted to terminate me but did not have the wherewithal or the heart to do so and how she singlehandedly raised me without a father and the whole nine yards."

"It's her whole life story. I'd rather not indulge you much more, as I promised myself after I read my mother's supposedly shameful secrets she revealed to me, not to repeat them. I did not have to know all this, but if it makes her feel better, then so be it. In my own heart, I've decided to keep the rest of it between the both of us. Please do not take this personally. It's just something I have to do. Maybe someday I will divulge the rest and her secret shame. I believe I have shared enough for you to understand, right, Rose?"

"Well, I can't say I disagree with you for not allowing me to read the actual letter for myself. I can certainly understand the trust and confidence she had in you, her only son, and I applaud you for your decency and ethics." Rose paused, unclasped his hand, and sat back in her chair.

"From what you've divulged, that is indeed her past, which is not beneficial to either of us right now, especially to you. Many parents try to avoid getting their children involved in their private lives and situations that they cannot alter. This sometimes makes the situation worse in the end. My advice to you is to let it go and pretend you never read it."

Rose paused and then spoke softly as though remembering some deeply hidden pain. "She has relieved herself of that guilt, which she carried for a long time. Now she is free. The Bible states, 'Confession is good for the soul.' She confesses to you, and I do believe her soul is at peace."

Rose slowly unfolded the paper containing the will and proceeded to read in silence first as Peter reclined somewhat in his chair, holding on to his glass of wine. He stared at Rose in curiosity, squinting suspiciously as he tried to read Rose's expression as she read silently. She took a few minutes to read the will over and over, not fully grasping its contents. Then she glanced at Peter, trying to communicate her understanding with her eyes. She was beyond belief and in a state of astonishment, almost out of her wits, when she saw the different categories of Peter's inheritance.

From all indications, this was not handwritten. It was all well prepared by the bank, and a copy was given to Peter's mom, which she gave to her pastor for safekeeping, assuming the original remained with the bank. By then, tears were flowing down Rose's cheeks unchecked. Her head pounded, and her heart raced with a fury within her chest. "This is amazing," she said.

Peter was transfixed across the table and was afraid to ask what the contents were. Finally, he nervously reached across the table, took hold of Rose's hands, and just held them there. "Can you please tell me what's in the will?" Peter asked.

The tears were still visible when Rose spoke. "Peter, don't be overconcerned with the secrets your mother hid from you for the years she did. Never mind the resentments she mentioned she encountered during her young life and having you out of marriage," she continued, "and the many reasons she kept her life's intriguing journey hidden. Every fiber of her love and what was left for her is in this will.

"Peter, all the legacy that was willed over to her from her adoptive parents, Mr. and Mrs. Joseph Swazi, she kept. She had not squandered any of it; she had it all these years, and it is securely kept in the bank." Rose was still astounded to know that, with all her wealth and good fortune, Peter's mother lived a comfortable yet humble life. She seemed to have maintained a balance in which she made Peter's welfare her sole goal in life. "Peter, it is all here. Yes, it all belongs to you now."

He still had no idea what the content of the will was. Peter stood up unsteadily to somehow ease the tension; however, they continued holding hands across the table as Rose spoke. Her tears now turned to laughter. Her eyes were filled with smiles in the ecstasy of a celebratory mood.

In that moment of exuberance, they tipped the wine bottle over, causing a deafening sound as the bottle hit the tiled floor with a resounding whack. The waiter came running over and, in an apologetic flurry, cleaned it up. Others sitting at various tables were alarmed at the sudden commotion. Peter and Rose were unaware that they were now the center of attention.

To that point, Peter had not heard the amount of his wealth. He still had a puzzled look on his face, not knowing what they were celebrating right now.

"Peter," she whispered, "you have inestimable riches. You are now not just a rich man. You are not just a man of means or merely someone who can afford to own your own domain. You are more than a billionaire. You have inherited the best inheritance a mother could ever have willed over to her son."

Rose swooned on and on. "Congratulations. *Out of evil*, God has provided this unsurmountable blessing." Rose was careful not to appear overexuberant but wanted to express her absolute joy over Peter's good fortune. They embraced for quite a while and hadn't noticed that almost everyone in the restaurant was driven to tears when they overheard the blessing that was bestowed on a son well deserving of it. Cheers came from everywhere; some couples walked over, introduced themselves, and wished Peter the very best.

He was never the type to be reckless with expenditure; he was always making a conscious effort to make good use of his finances. Now, with this added legacy, along with the ability God had given him, the sky would not even limit him. They celebrated again with more wine, and this time, they spoke only above a whisper so they would not further disturb the others' dining.

To change the subject for a while, Peter spoke again of calling his boss the next day and requesting more time. "I would sure hope he would concede."

"So what if he doesn't?" Rose said with a grin and handed Peter the envelopes, and then she looked at her watch. "Do you mind if we go, Peter? I have a few job interviews tomorrow, and I need to prepare myself. Please, Peter, try sleeping for once. Your struggles are over. Plus, you could use an awe moment alone."

Peter paid the check with his debit card, and they were on their way. There were cabs waiting outside the Hilton as usual for regular late-night restaurant diners. This time, Peter and Rose walked out holding hands for the first time. Peter had a comforting smile that one could tell; he was celebrating something in spite of his unexpected loss.

The moment they sat in the taxi, Peter asked Rose the contents of the will. She was happy to share every word of what was there. Peter was flabbergasted; he probably thought Rose was overreacting. He was almost sure it was not as enormous as she demonstrated. He was spaced out; all the way to Rose's house, he never spoke a word but kept looking through the window of the taxi.

When they arrived, Rose asked, "Are you okay, Peter?"

"Yes, I am okay," Peter responded. "I am just trying to digest all that you have said. I am now in a better position to read the document and figure out what my next move will be."

Rose cautioned that he should take care of himself as she stepped from the taxi. Peter lived closer to the Hilton but had to accompany Rose to see her getting in.

"Thanks for dinner. Please call me when you are home."

"Sure, Rose, I will."

Rose's usual custom was, after the day's activities, she would make herself a drink whenever she walked into the house. This time, she ignored that ritual and, for whatever reason, walked down the hallway leading to her bedroom, where she had hanging wall pictures of her parents. With a long and solid gaze, she wondered if they had ever secured any of their wealth for her. They must have had some kind of investment, 401(k), personal savings, or some kind of share. She mulled it over and over.

I am going to investigate my parents' holdings if this is the last thing I do. I have a premonition that there is something stashed away, Rose surmised. *I know they both died at an early age, and of course, the newspapers and media proved it true, but that could not just be the be-all and end-all of my parents. They had to have something of worth somewhere.*

The reports I read said they were executives of a major hedge fund company on Wall Street. I knew I was their only child but had never searched out the history or background of them, which I regrettably ignored, and I should have when I became an adult. I just took it for granted that all I should be concerned with was how to survive and to be contented with what my aunt, Stella, gave me. *In a few weeks, I will be twenty-two years old. I've graduated college with a bachelor's degree in banking and finance, and I've also a degree in theology from the School of Theological Seminary of California.*

Rose continued to allow her imagination to run wild as if she was dreaming. *After their death, I was automatically taken by Aunt Stella, who had no family other than my father, Mark, who has been dead for a number of years now. She raised and took care of me until I was through with my education and made the decision to move to Boca.*

Rose Alexander, yeah, that's my name, she mused as she lay back on the bed. *I will now sort myself out appropriately.* She was impelled by Peter's inheritance and thought she might just have a fortune herself.

Each day, Rose became more and more curious about her parents' financial status and thought she might just strike gold. Rose remembered how she became distraught after college and felt there should be a much better way to a brighter future. Remembering the light bulb, she got to relocate to Boca Raton, where she would try to make a fresh start in a new environment and make new friends. She thought of the years spent going to schools, from high school to college to university.

Those were the years she looked back at, thinking, *Why hasn't anything ever crossed my mind about my parents' financial status? Maybe because I had won a full scholarship that includes books and so on. Plus, my aunt had been very supportive of me, making sure I was well-equipped for my schooling.*

She reminisced about how she sent out loads of résumés and job applications, targeting various companies, hoping to find employment but to no avail. *I would grab hold of the Sunday Times as soon as it comes off the press, carefully going through the Want Ad sections, hoping to find something to do. A group of my friends and I would do a more in-*

depth job search on the internet on weekends, hoping that on Monday morning, we would have new applications to submit, but everything turned up thumbs-down.

The failures were too many and had become tiring. She thought God had forgotten her and thought her prayers were in vain. Up to the time of making the decision to change her environment, it had not crossed her thoughts to inquire about her parents' fortune.

Chapter 3

The house Rose purchased was with the money she saved from odd summer jobs here and there during college and the savings she had from what Aunt Stella allowed her because she had no overhead expenses. She was carried away, deep in thought, rehashing most of her past, and she hadn't heard the phone ring. She began to wonder why Peter hadn't called also.

Just then, there was another ring, and it was Peter. "I was a little concerned, Rose, when you didn't answer. You had me worried much."

"I am fine," Rose replied. "I was just reflecting a bit and got carried away."

"Okay, we'll talk in the morning after I speak with my boss. Rest well."

Rose stayed awake almost all night, trying to decide whether she should engage an attorney to handle the investigation of her parents' investments, if any, and if there were, maybe try executing it herself. She thought of calling her aunt, Stella, to ask if she had any knowledge of her parents' wealth and her opinion or suggestion in pursuing it. All sorts of thoughts went through her head during the night until she could plainly see the sun coming up.

By then, Peter had rehashed the will again on his own time and continued to be dumbfounded. He lay on his mother's bed, staring at the ceiling in awe and astonishment. His mother had bequeathed quite a hearty legacy to him; this would last for as long as he wanted it to. He would not be in need of anything in many years to come.

Saint Paul's Cathedral was not mentioned to receive any of his inheritance. Ms. Swazi had attached a separate note of a hefty sum, asking Peter to deliver it to Father Hurling, thanking him for his counseling and efforts in seeing to it she was always okay. And she also left a small amount to the church's orphanage, where she volunteered.

Peter immediately thought he would contact his attorney to meet with him first to discuss the procedure and then make an appointment with the bank managers. He wanted to make sure everything in all aspects was in proper perspective and that the allocation was legally done.

He was still wearing the clothes he wore to dinner when Peter realized the sun was shining through his mother's bedroom window. That was when he remembered he needed to have the windows repaired. Since the storm, it was just temporarily boarded up. Everything happened so quickly with his mom's death and the funeral that he didn't have the time to call the repair company. He sat up, a bit disoriented, trying to focus. "I have to call my boss, Raymond," Peter said, hoping he'd agree to more bereavement time.

Peter's cell phone rang. It was Rose, making sure he was up and also reminding him to make the call. "I will call you back," said Peter. He was about to make the call when Rose interrupted.

For a minute, Peter waited to develop the fortitude he needed to speak with Raymond Castro. He prayed, hoping his request would be granted without any trepidation. "Hello, Raymond. This is Peter from the Central Wing Aviation base. I know I've already had a few weeks off previously due to the death of my mother. Remember we spoke yesterday?"

"Oh yes, Peter, how are you doing?"

"Not totally fine at all," Peter responded. "When we spoke yesterday, I thought I would have been physically and mentally ready to return to my flying duties today, but I will not be able to. I have some very important paperwork that needs my immediate attention, such as filing my mother's death certificate with the city and other paperwork I cannot overlook at this time. Plus, the enormity of grasping my mother's sudden death is just too much right now. I had not thought of these things until my attorney pointed out all the things I needed to do."

Raymond listened in silence as Peter thoroughly explained the types of proceedings he had to complete that had to do with his mother's passing. "Well..." Raymond sighed. "We will see how well we can shuffle around a few of the other pilots and hope they will comply. You know the flying rules. We are not allowed to schedule anyone for more than the required hours. I will call a few of our reserves and ask that they stand by. When do you think you'll be able to return to work?"

"Another two weeks should do it, Raymond. By then, I should be done."

"Okay, Peter, that should be fine."

Peter was joyful at the end of the conversation, feeling somewhat relaxed in his mind. He made himself a cup of coffee as he dialed Rose. By that time, she was on her way to her first interview.

"Hello, Rose. I got the approval for two more weeks. Can we meet over dinner tonight so we can discuss a few things and see where we go from here? And we'll talk about the will also."

"Why do you need me to be a part of the discussion of the will, Peter? I want you to make the appointment with your attorney first. I do believe he will be better able to point you in the right direction."

"I know all of what you are saying, Rose, but you are now a part of me. You have become an integral ingredient in my life, and I refuse to go any further without involving you in my plans or allow anything to distract that, okay? So, are you accepting my invitation or not?" Peter said it with a purposeful note of command in his voice.

"Okay, Peter, you win. I will meet you later for dinner."

That night, they decided to have dinner in Chinatown at one of the quaint areas of dining in Boca Raton. The food was always different there, and there was always a line no matter what time or what type of meal was desired. As usual, Peter picked Rose up at seven o'clock; this time, she was picked up and chauffeur-driven in a boyish way by Peter himself so she could enjoy and feel like a VIP from the back seat. He decided to rent this car so he would not have to worry about taking a taxi, especially during this time when he had so many businesses to take care of. His mother had just sold her car and was in negotiation for a new Toyota Camry from Ben's Dealers in Lower Boca.

"How nice!" Rose exclaimed as she stepped into the red upholstered Bentley. "I did not know dealers rent Bentleys. I thought these luxury cars were only owned by the rich and famous."

"No, Rose, these cars are also reserved for anyone who can afford them." Peter sped off with lightning speed as they needed to have dinner and be done at a reasonable time. Rose was having a second interview the next morning and needed to be prepared.

"Yes," Peter continued, "this company deals with various rentals, but mainly Bentleys and Benzes. It was not expensive with my discount from the Air Force. Besides, this executive-only rental is owned by a group of retired Air Force men from the early sixties. I used to rent from them a while back whenever I was here to see Mom. It's a nice car to drive. Plus, I thought I might do something nice for us this evening instead of a taxi."

Over dinner, Peter read the will for himself again and was still at a loss seeing all that was now his. He even discussed retiring from the Air Force with the possibility of owning a business. The financial aspect of the will was more than he could spend in a lifetime. The house was in both their names, along with other estates his mother inherited from her adoptive German parents. The Swiss accounts with stocks and bonds, shares, and local bank accounts, to name a few that were willed to her, had all been transferred over to Peter.

"With all this," Peter said with a look of relief, "I will not be able to use up this inheritance even when I am old and gray. This is a rather pleasant surprise." He showed a wealthy grin. "If things hadn't happened the way they did, I would not have the foggiest idea of what was laid aside for me. My mother was almost a recluse, living with the appearance of a hand-to-mouth existence, getting involved with only a few social events while she volunteered at the church. She had no visitors except brief gestures to the neighbors that were few and far between. During Thanksgiving and Christmas festivities, she would volunteer to bake a couple of turkeys to help feed the homeless and those who could not afford food for the holidays, the less fortunate, and also do bake sales for the children's cantata."

Dinner was now served; it was shrimp marinara over noodles seeped in garlic sauce, which they totally enjoyed. Toward the end of dinner, Peter thought they could also see the latest movie that everyone talked about over the last few weeks, *Left Behind*. Rose thought it would be a good idea, but this time, she declined as she was scheduled for another interview at nine o'clock in the morning.

After all, Peter knew he just wanted to have a little more time with Rose as, somehow, he was beginning to feel affection toward her. Naturally, he had other friends and close associates before meeting Rose on that stormy night. As destiny would have it, the way they met and what happened afterward brought about a bond between them.

Yes, destiny closed in on two lives that came together when nature stepped in, when the mystery of divine intervention waltzed in on that stormy night when there was no choice, no alternative, no place else to go. Yes, this was a moment that was inevitable; this was when the golden parachute fell, and at the bottom, two separate lives hung. This metamorphosis was now steadily in progress, and soon, a chrysalis would birth a butterfly.

They left the restaurant at about ten o'clock as Peter slowly drove her home. This time, he did not see her in but walked her to the door. Rose had rehearsed her good-night speech and was ready to make it as soon as she got to her door. But to her amazement, Peter invited himself in.

"Don't you think it's a bit late, Peter? I need to be up early tomorrow for my next interview, and I'm feeling a bit tired."

"Sit down, Rose. There is something I must tell you."

Rose got quite anxious and wondered, *What now?* They had dinner for almost two hours, and she thought they had discussed all that there was to be discussed. There was a mysterious look on Peter's face that was rather intriguing.

"Rose, I... I... don't know how to say this, but I have to. I am aware we met only a short while ago, and during the unexpected death of my mom, without asking, you stood with me. I know we are still in the 'getting to know you' phase, but now, as you can see, I have quite a bit on my hands with no one to share with. I will be back to work soon, and while I am gone, there are some important businesses that I need someone close to keep an eye on.

"As strange as this might sound and as mysterious as it looks, I have no hidden agenda, no reservations whatsoever, but I have fallen in love with you so much that I must ask, will you marry me?" By then, Peter's eyes welled up with tears; the sincerity in them was unmistakable. He got on his knees and, holding Rose's hand, placed a beautiful diamond engagement ring on her finger as she looked on with incredulity from the couch where she sat.

"Will you marry me, Rose? I love you so much. Say something, please, Rose. Please?"

Out of Evil

By this time, Rose had tears of unbelief running down her cheeks. She tried to decipher the words she just heard, wondering if it was a dream.

"Talk back to me, Rose. Will you spend the rest of your life with me? I need you, Rose."

It was then, with a soft voice of utter surprise and bliss, that she said, "Yes, Peter, I will spend the rest of my life with you. I will marry you." Rose was elated that the turn of events was beginning to be realized in a matter of a few months. When she moved from New York, she had no idea what life would throw at her; her entire focus was getting a job to work her way to success. She knew she was starting a whole new subsistence; therefore, she began to familiarize herself with the new environment. She also joined the public library, where she could meet new people, as well as the swim club, the block association, and even the Young Women's Christian Association.

A few weeks after Rose had purchased her house, she was invited to an auction of some Baldwin grand pianos and organs in the music store a few blocks from the church. Although she did not know the first note to play, she made a bid on a beautiful Hammond organ and won; she purchased it anyway. The moment she said yes to Peter, he walked over to the piano, which was situated in the far corner of the large living room, lifted the cover, and began playing one of the most beautiful songs that was ever written by Elisha A. Hoffman and Anthony J. Showalter, resulting from the scripture they had meditated on moments earlier, "Leaning on the Everlasting Arms."[3]

Peter learned to play the piano as a child in Sunday school and continued during high school and college, even after graduation. He loved music so much that he found time to play outside of work. He was so proficient on the keyboard. This masterpiece of a song he also learned by going to church with his mother was one of her favorites.

---

3   Hoffman, Elisha A., and Anthony J. Showalter. "Leaning on the Everlasting Arm." 1887.

Not only was Peter playing the song, but in the late hour, he also softly sang the verse.

What a fellowship, what a joy divine
Leaning on the everlasting arms
What a blessedness, what a peace is mine
Leaning on the everlasting arms.

Rose walked over and sat next to Peter on the piano stool, placed her head on his shoulder, and whispered in his ear, "What have I to dread, what have I to fear, leaning on the everlasting arms, I have blessed peace with my Lord so near, leaning on the everlastings arms."

That was the moment they were both waiting for without even knowing it, a moment of revelation, a moment of strength, confessing to each other they had known the love of God. Rose's encounter with God was somewhat strange. Although she was active at the church in New York, she realized then that knowing Christ was much more than just being active.

She told Peter about that memorable afternoon when she visited Saint Paul's Cathedral after seeing that huge painting of Jesus Christ with His arms stretched toward the lost sheep. She said, "I felt I was lost, and Jesus said, 'Come.' I asked Jesus into my heart, and I know He did receive me. My life changed, and I could not explain it. I only know I was different from that moment on."

Peter looked at Rose in astonishment as she revealed to him her encounter with God. With the melody of the song in his eyes, Peter said, "I have been to Saint Paul's almost all my life from a child. It is our worship center. I know I'm grown and have gone my own way, but I have never forgotten that this is my foundation. When I had weekends off from flying, I would always attend church with Mom, but I had never scrutinized that magnificent painting till the evening of her funeral.

"I sat waiting for the funeral service to begin as I looked intently around the sanctuary, reading and observing every decor and writing over and over when my eyes suddenly focused on what I believe God divinely wanted me to see. In my bereavement, I saw His hand reaching out for me. Yes, Rose, I knew that He wanted to hold me and let me know it was going to be okay.

"At that moment, a delicious feeling of tranquility came over me. I was afraid to say it, Rose. You may have wondered how it is I am able to be so strong. Each time I think of Mother, who prayed for me, and her efforts to make a life for herself and me, I get a feeling of comfort. But more than all, had I not met God in Saint Paul's that evening, things would have been much different. I knew there was a correlation between us. I prayed, asking God to reveal this to both of us, and He did."

It was already two o'clock in the morning when Peter looked at his watch and exclaimed, "Oh, I am so sorry, Rose! I had no idea it was this late."

Rose was still in shock from the proposal and was busy getting her thoughts together. Time was the last thing she would be paying attention to. In fact, time stood still in that moment as Peter wrapped his arms around her as if he would never let her go. He finally pulled her from him, placed a warm kiss squarely on her lips, patted her shoulders, walked across the room, picked up his jacket, and headed for the door. "We'll talk tomorrow, Rose. Then we'll decide where we go from here. Thanks for accepting my proposal, okay?"

Between the foyer and the entrance doorway, he had taken no more than a few steps when, suddenly, he held his head and crouched to the floor. There was blood gushing from his nostrils. "Peter! Peter!" Rose screamed, ran over, pulled him to her, and then helped him to the couch. He was conscious and alert. In the meantime, she dialed 911, and they responded immediately. Though very nervous and anxious, she was able to provide her home address along with other important information.

Peter felt he was just very tired and really needed some time off. Rose was busy making sure he remained conscious and awake. The ambulance was there within seven minutes, and the paramedics attended to him quickly and quite professionally. They predicted that it was just a simple nosebleed and that the doctors would probably say the same. They assured Rose he would be fine, but routinely, they needed to take him to the emergency room for further observation.

After a few hours of routine check, the doctors did diagnose a nosebleed, as the paramedics had mentioned, but decided they would keep him a little while longer for further observation. Rose seemed a bit scared but tried to keep her composure, even though it could be seen that she was visibly shaken. The nurse who took Peter's vital signs noticed the pale look on her face and quietly consulted with the team of doctors to see if she could check Rose's vital signs as well. But she was fine; her blood pressure was a little elevated, and they gave her a one-time dose of Norvasc, tested her again later that afternoon, and told her she was okay.

Eventually, the doctors gave Peter a clean bill of health. They signed the discharge papers right away and advised him to take some time for a vacation of rest and relaxation. Peter knew he had been burning the candles on both ends from the time of his mom's accident and death that he really needed to calm down and unwind for a few days.

In the meantime, Rose hailed a cab as she waited for Peter to walk out. "Where are we going?" Rose asked.

"To your house, Rose," Peter responded. "I need a few hours to loosen up, and I think you too."

Like déjà vu, Rose recalled it was just a few weeks ago that Peter's mom was carried from their home by the same paramedics to Boca General Hospital. It was hard then for her to control her emotions;

she was all in tears. "I can't go to my appointment later, Peter," Rose said, glancing at him as he sat back in a relaxed mood in the back seat of the taxi. It was almost seven o'clock in the morning; she was quite sure it would be okay with Peter but still wanted to get his opinion. They had spent all night in the emergency room.

"I will notify them at 8:45 and ask them if they could reschedule the appointment. I want to be near you now, Peter, if that's okay with you. You gave me such a scare earlier that I would hate to know anything like that ever occurs again. Maybe it was a good idea you invited yourself in," Rose said with a smile. "Or you would be up a creek without a paddle, Peter." She wore a broader grin.

Of course, Peter knew Rose was just very happy about her engagement and, after everything, to see him recover from the nosebleed. Peter, as though he was plotting a course, stared at Rose. She had never seen him this serious. He gave her the chills, and then he spoke. "Apart from me falling in love with you, I find it rather scary to be alone. I would have been with Mom here on my day off if, God forbid, I fell ill. What if I was alone at home? Now she is gone, and you are all I have. You see why I asked you to marry me last night, Rose. I want you not only near me, not only in times like this but also to be the one with whom I wish to share the rest of my life." With a consoling smile, he thanked Rose profusely for her kindness and thoughtfulness. Peter again proposed a second time within twenty-four hours.

Before they knew it, the day had passed. It was already three o'clock in the afternoon; the day was almost over to do any business at all. Peter said, "I'll relax for a couple of hours. We could call for an order of some assortment of Chinese food; I'm starved. How about you, Rose? I'm sure you must be famished, too. Is there any nonalcoholic wine in the house for us to celebrate with?"

"Who would want to have nonalcoholic wine to celebrate with, Peter? Even at the Lord's Supper, the wine has alcohol to celebrate and memorialize the death, burial, and resurrection of our Lord Jesus Christ," Rose said jokingly. "I will most certainly call for Chinese food, Peter. While you go home and get refreshed, I will prepare the dinner setting and be ready for us to celebrate as soon as you are back. How about you give us about an hour and a half? That should be enough time."

Peter's rented Bentley was still parked out front. On his way out, he shouted, "Oh my! I was not thinking, Rose. I can pick up the wine on my way back. Do you need anything else added to our celebration?"

"No, you go ahead. I will be waiting. Be careful."

He then hurried out and drove off cautiously.

It was exactly one hour and a half when there was a knock at the door. Peter did not wait for Rose to open it because the door was already unlocked anyway; therefore, he was able to let himself in. Rose was already dressed in a soft evening violet-blue dress that was her Mom's and was now able to fit her so beautifully. Peter was extremely taken aback by Rose's appearance, and without warning, he held her close and kissed her passionately. He then gasped for air and asked, "Are we going somewhere?"

"No, remember, we are having Chinese food. It's waiting." She spoke with such poise and grace and then calmly walked across the hall to the organ. This time, she was not accompanying Peter in a song, but he was. Without Peter's knowledge, Rose had started online piano lessons as a surprise to him. She sat elegantly at the piano, opened an old hymnal, and began playing with a flourish as she sang the beautiful hymn:

Amazing grace! How sweet the sound
That saved a wretch like me!
I once was lost but now am found,
Was blind, but now I see.

Through many dangers, toils, and snares,
I have already come;
'Tis grace that brought me safe thus far,
And grace will lead me home.[4]

The room was now filled with the presence of God, and it was like a holy hush engulfed the atmosphere. Peter and Rose began praying for fifteen minutes as if they had rehearsed. At the end of the prayer, they were both drenched in tears as they spoke to God, acknowledging Him using a language only He could understand. When the Holy Spirit was through, and they were able to think apart from that endowment out loud, they thanked God for His presence as He, in essence, exposed a sanctioning bond between them. Peter seemed to draw strength from that encounter; he had always consciously remembered to give thanks.

They held hands and walked to the dining area. To his amazement, Rose had decorated the table with fresh flowers and fruits. Besides, the Chinese food was dished into fine china and placed on a warmer. They enjoyed a sumptuous meal with candles lit and a few gulps of wine with loud laughter while reminiscing on what had happened, and with much prayer, they hoped there would not be another occurrence.

It was obvious that they were tired and weary, and Rose found it hard to ask Peter if he would be leaving soon. In as much as she would love for him to stay, she was governed by the same Christian ethics. It was as though Peter read her thoughts when he immediately stood, gave a tired grin, kissed Rose on the forehead, and then headed for the door.

"Good night, Rose," he said with his arms around her shoulders. "I will call you in the morning. We have a lot to talk

---

4   Lifeway Worship. "Amazing Grace! How Sweet the Sound." *Top 100 Hymns.* 2018.

about. I think it's about time we make a conscious decision on what our future should look like." Peter kissed her again, slipped through the door, got in the rented Bentley, and slowly drove away.

Chapter 4

It was a long day after such an ordeal with Peter, and being at the hospital, they were both exhausted. Peter called as soon as he was home and promised he would take a late-morning nap and would call her as soon as he was awakened and dressed.

Rose was up at the crack of dawn, delving into her second cup of coffee, when there was a knock on the door. To her surprise, it was her aunt, Stella, from New York. She had arrived the day before but had been busy with her friends who came along with her on business. "Come in," Rose said as she welcomed her to Boca. "Why didn't you call to alert me of your trip? I would have made ample preparation for you." Rose was so excited to see her only living relative that she could hardly restrain herself.

"Oh, Rose, this is just a doctor's visit. I will come again to spend more time slated just for you later in the year. My friends are waiting for me outside. Here, your letters have been coming back to your old address, no such number. It seemed they had a wrong address, and these seemed very important, Rose. They are all from the law firm of Klaus and Glasgow, and as I had this trip planned, I decided to bring them along. You have a beautiful house, Rose. I love it. Please do enjoy it. You are well deserving."

Both ladies chatted briefly as Aunt Stella exited quickly and promised to call her later. The letters were left on the side of an antique wooden table when they parted. Rose hurried to the waiting taxi for her second interview.

It all went well, and this time, she was offered the position of executive administrator to Carl Moorhead, who was the head of operations at one of Boca's largest hedge fund companies, Black Pearl, situated in Delray Beach. Her interviewer, Mr. Harry Roberts, admired her for her charming demeanor, look of honesty, and business attire. This would be Rose's first real job since graduating from college; she was approved immediately and was asked to take the position right away, as early as three days. With a grin of acceptance, they both shook hands. Rose was asked to go directly to human resources so she could complete the newly hired paperwork.

In spite of the acquisition of this new position, there was a look of sadness captured in Rose's smile when she met Peter that evening for dinner, and as much as she tried to masquerade her feelings, it was quite obvious that she was not all excited reporting to Peter the results of the interview. Peter had detected that something was not quite right as he read into her half-hearted greeting. He saw there was something wrong and insisted that she share it. "I got the job, Peter, and I'm starting on Monday morning," she blurted out.

"Oh, that's good news, Rose, except I don't think you will be working there for any length of time, maybe just a few weeks."

There was a minute of silence before Rose's response. "I think I understand what you are implying, Peter, but I am not yet in the position you are insinuating legally. I have no legal claims to you. I have no legal rights. We have only been engaged.

"You have asked me to marry you, but until we have done so, please, Peter, let me be. Let me do this assignment for some time. I will be gainfully employed and not be portrayed as a freeloader just because you have gotten the means to support me. Now is a time of much prayer, where we continue to ask God's divine guidance in our lives.

"I know you need me now and that we have gotten used to spending much time together, but this needs conscious thinking and planning, and we need to be really levelheaded. This will be my first real job, Peter. I trust you will understand. It's all because I love you so much. I would certainly hate to hop onto your coattails and spoil or tarnish our future, whichever way it takes us. I just really would like to work for myself for a while. Please, Peter?"

"Rose, have you listened to yourself? You are making absolutely no sense. Have you forgotten what we have talked about? I am aware that this is your first real job, and already, you have secured yourself in it above all that we had previously talked about.

"What has gotten into you, Rose? Do you really trust me and all that I have told you? We are now engaged to be married. All the cards are on the table. You know everything up to the smallest details so far. I am disappointed in your behavior, Rose. You are putting me in an awkward position."

There was an uneasy silence after Rose made her speech. They got through dinner, not communicating, not glancing at each other, and not even sporadically giving a touch of togetherness. At the end of dinner, they were immediately ready to part for the evening as there was so much on each of their proverbial plates to plan and pray about.

Rose got out of the car with just a mere "Good night. Thanks for dinner. Rest well."

"Thanks," Peter barely muttered.

Rose barely closed the door when Peter drove off, a bit enraged. He was confused about all that transpired between them and the sudden wave of differences so obvious between them.

It was six o'clock on Monday morning when the doorbell rang. Rose had already showered and was half-dressed. She rushed to the door; it was Peter. "I am here to take you to your first day of work," he said with a sheepish smile, hugging Rose and assuring her it would be all right. Peter apologized for his silence at dinner the night before. He said that after he got into bed, he thought of how selfish he was.

With a sigh of relief, Rose mentioned she could have acted better herself, and she, too, was very sorry. They both decided that the kind of childish behavior displayed last evening would not happen again. Her imagination ran wild during the forty-minute ride, which seemed to take forever. Then she couldn't help reminiscing on the activities in her life leading up to this point, going a long way back down memory lane and even down the path of decision.

As fate would have it, there were storm warnings again as Rose remembered the terrible loss that Peter suffered just months ago. The rains had not let up all day, and there was flooding everywhere. Very often, the weather reporters were cautioning everyone to be alert and adhere. On the night she met Peter, she ignored the warnings to take her umbrella. Even if she had it, it would not be of much use considering the wind that accompanied the rain. Warnings were given of possible tornadoes, and all should take precautions. At least they were alert and conscious of their surroundings and warned to be careful.

Peter and Rose met without any advance notice, unbeknownst to either of them, only to God because He knows the paths that we take. He will guide us with His eyes. These are the great hidden secrets that God shows and reveals when He is ready. But there are criteria that must meet the requirements of God, who so lavishly provides for His own.

The greatest weapon that can chart the paths and future of those whose lives are hidden with Christ in God is prayer. The strangest things will unfold where we least expect them. Sometimes, the direction we take doesn't usually lead us the way we desire. Giving God a chance to chart our course and having a humble heart, without warning, there goes the dawn of a new day. "Seek ye first the kingdom of God" (Matthew 6:33, KJV).

The first day of work went well as Rose familiarized herself with the office setting, the staff, and the managing directors. This was her lineup for the most part of the morning. One of the associates took her for a grand tour of the entire facility. She became most interested in the cafeteria as she would have to keep the stock there and do the orders when needed. This part of the job description was certainly not something Rose had an interest in, but she needed a start.

It was noon, and the office closed its operations for one hour. Rose, with anxious steps, rushed to the elevator and headed to the main lobby, where she could speak to Peter privately. "Hi, Pete. How are you? I can't wait to tell you about my day so far." Rose rambled on and on; there was, sure enough, an odd feeling of a new environment, so there was a lot to talk about.

There were various newspaper stands crowding the cash-out area with a number of soda machines, candies, all sorts of chips, cigar paraphernalia, and an assortment of books. While speaking to Peter, Rose's eyes roamed around; she was transfixed with the headlines of the *Washington Post*, which read, "Eastern Airlines Has Filed Bankruptcy." "Oh my goodness, Peter, have you seen the news?"

"Yes," Peter responded. "I wanted to call you all morning but was afraid I would not be able to talk with you the first day on the job. I am glad you called. I have seen the *Washington Post*. How unbelievable! I have been calling Raymond, but he's not picking up his extension. This is utter nonsense. I think I will take a trip to Fairchild Air Force Base in Washington, where I work out, tomorrow to find out what this is all about, but we will talk about it later when you are home. What time do you leave today?"

"Oh, I leave at five."

"I'll pick you up then."

Later, as Rose walked out the double glass doors of Black Pearl and Associates, there was Peter waiting, still driving the rented red Bentley, which gave everyone cause to notice as they went by. "Peter, I am getting too used to this luxury. I think it's time to return this car," Rose said with a grin.

"I have decided to buy it, Rose, as a gift to you for accepting my proposal to be my wife." Peter was looking at Rose with a thankful smile as he roared off.

"Oh, for Christ's sake, you didn't, did you?"

"Yes, I did, Rose. It was during my negotiation at the dealer that I found out about my company going bankrupt."

"So why did you go through buying the car, Peter? Do you think you need to have this now?"

"Oh, Rose, give me one good reason why you think we cannot afford to have this car now. I would have included you in the process, but it's a surprise. So, should I return it?" Peter said with a grin. "What do you say?"

For the first time in a long time, Rose was at a loss for words. She could not believe this Bentley was actually hers. "Thank you so much, Peter. I don't know how else to say thanks."

Peter's response was, "You are most welcome, and thanks for accepting my gift."

Rose looked at him with a questionable gesture as if to say, *You are something else.*

"I am meeting with some of the guys from my job that live in Boca in about an hour to discuss where we go from here before I fly down to Washington tomorrow. I would like you to come with me. This would be a fine time to meet some of the people I worked with for so many years. Can you, please?"

"Okay, I will, Peter. I only need a few minutes to freshen up," she said as they drove to Rose's house.

"I'll wait here in the car. Please do hurry."

In a few minutes, Rose was back in the Bentley wearing a more casual but elegant outfit that fit the occasion. "Hmm, are you Superman? You certainly got out of work clothes and into that elegant dress fast enough, young lady." Peter leaned over, kissed her forehead, and headed downtown.

The drive was about an hour already when Peter stopped and collected a small package from a store a little behind where he stopped. Rose tried to see where he had gone, but his return was surprisingly quick, and she had not enough time. The package he picked up was shoved in the trunk, and there was no explanation about what it was, and Rose did not ask.

They arrived at what seemed like an exotic restaurant from the outside, and Rose observed a well-dressed, hurrying, bustling group of people gathering at the entrance to one of the halls. It seemed they were waiting to be seated. A waiter met Peter at the door and spoke to him softly. Rose tried eavesdropping but was not able to hear a single word of what was said. She did not question Peter; all she knew and believed was what he told her, him meeting his friends to discuss the airline going under and possible transfers to other airlines and Air Force bases.

It was not long before the doors were opened, and Rose could see everyone moving forward to be seated. They must have waited in the car for about ten minutes when Peter was signaled in. As they approached the huge glass doors that swung open on both sides, she could see the reflections of people standing on a huge bandstand as if waiting for someone to wave them when to begin.

As they walked in, there it was. Everyone was standing, and the band struck up loud music, playing "And Now the Time Has Come." Rose wondered if she was hallucinating or if this was for real. There was a man standing at the podium who announced, "Ladies and gentlemen, may I have your attention? I would like to present to you Mr. Peter Swazi."

Then, someone hurried over to the couple and showed Rose a chair where she could sit. She watched in awe as Peter made his way to the podium. His face was glowing in a way that she had never seen before, with such an infectious smile that the whole room lit up and was smiling at him as he spoke.

"I thank all of you for coming this afternoon at such short notice, but that's what friends are for. Most of you know me for quite some time and have frequently questioned me about where I will be heading." Peter continued by saying, "And for those of us who have worked with this particular airline and have heard the sad news of the company closing down due to the rising economy and, of course, other detriments, I wish all of us a brighter future and hope we will find employment elsewhere as soon as possible."

"Unfortunately, as most of you will well remember, I lost my mom a few weeks ago in that terrible storm when a tree fell on our home, smashing through her bedroom window and crushing her, almost killing her instantly. That same night, I met a beautiful young woman by the name of Rose Alexander, a born New Yorker." As Peter mentioned her name, he beckoned to one of the ushers to help Rose to the podium.

Rose's eyes were filled with incomprehension, trying to decipher what this was all about; she was escorted to stand next to Peter. The minute she got to him, as he continued speaking, he made the incredible announcement. "Ladies and gentlemen, a few days ago, I asked this beautiful young woman to be my bride. My first proposal was done behind closed doors when I presented her with this unusual cut of a diamond engagement ring." Peter held up Rose's hand and showed everyone the ring. "But this evening, I would like for everyone to share with me the joy of my newfound love."

Everyone gasped with excitement and stood with thunderous applause, which went on for about three minutes. Rose could not hold back the tears. Peter reached into his pocket, pulled out a small white box that he opened in a hurry, popped out an unusual pearl necklace, and put it around Rose's neck. Everyone continued cheering with shouts of congratulations when a sudden hush engulfed the room.

A woman came out of nowhere and pushed past the guard at the door with a bizarre look and a horrible attitude as her voice resounded. "He's mine!" she yelled. "You can't have him!"

"You will not interfere," she mentioned to Rose. "He didn't tell you he was already engaged?"

"Well, Peter, don't just stand there. Say something," she continued.

Peter froze, and so did everyone for a moment. Then, in astonishment, with a subdued voice, Peter calmly said, "Grace? Is this you? Or am I seeing a ghost? Where have you been? What happened? I was told you were dead in that deadly car crash that caught on fire five years ago when the car you were driving went out of control and flipped over a cliff in France and then burst into flames. Oh my God! Grace Milford?"

Pandemonium broke in the beautifully decorated room when the guards rushed toward Grace Milford and escorted her to the exit door, which was a few steps behind her. Some of the guests found it very amusing, while others were overconcerned about what this story was all about. Peter's best friend, Richard Azan, walked over and helped him to his seat on the dais. It was as though all his strength had disappeared as his world crumbled. Rose was already sitting, and there was an older woman handing her tissues and finding it difficult to calm her. This entire outburst happened so suddenly that no one was able to make rhyme or reason out of all of it.

In the meantime, the band made the best of a bad situation as they softly played various songs that would bring reassurance to the chaotic moment, also trying to bring back an evening that had started with excitement, love, and curiosity. Everyone's eyes were on Peter as if to say, *What are you waiting for? We need answers. We need an explanation.* But Peter was too traumatized to even try explaining.

One could hear her sobbing outside the exit door that led to a long corridor as Grace Milford walked, led away by the county sheriff, Thomas Wakefield, who was called by the restaurant's security shortly after she finagled her way in, pretending to be a guest who arrived late.

It took a long time for all to gather their composure, but to Peter's amazement, they all stayed in support of him and Rose. Peter was one of those guys who was friendly to every person he met, and his mantra was always, "If I can help somebody as I pass along, then my living will not be in vain."

Dinner was about to be served, and everyone was asked to be seated so the service could begin. The waiters were once again busy bringing in the salads and taking orders from the mouth-watering, well-organized entrée. "I will have you enjoy your meal." Peter stood quite calmly and spoke. "At the end, my explanation will be the dessert." This brought laughter, which broke the monotony and gave some comfort and stability to the curious mind.

In the meantime, Rose—as curious and shocked as she was and as much as her imagination ran wild, feeling hurt and in a spin of despair—behaved sensibly and in a mature manner, for which everyone commended her, along with her strong deportment and well-mannered action. Yes, she cried. Yes, she was surprised and felt deceived, but she waited for an explanation, like everyone else.

Rose regained her composure and then made her way to the podium; she calmly managed to get everyone's attention and asked that they please listen to the statement she was about to make. "What happened earlier came as a surprise to all of us. I am sure we will be hearing from my fiancé in a moment. Therefore, I will not be making much comments on that."

Everyone cheered with anticipation.

"Peter and I met under the weirdest conditions. Both of us have been praying for God to send someone in our lives who would become each other's soul mate. I am a born New Yorker to my parents, Mr. and Mrs. Mark Alexander, whom many of you older ones here may have heard and remembered. They were killed many years ago in a plane crash. I moved here from New York City after college in search of a different life. I am only twenty-two years old, with the desire to make the best of whatever comes my way."

"Over these few months, Peter and I have become inseparable and have vowed that our past lives would be left behind, especially the things that hurt us the most. I would like to thank Peter for his love and trust and for taking the step in asking me to be his bride. We have made new commitments and are desirous of your prayers. I don't think Peter deserved that kind of outburst. And because of what I just saw and heard, we ask for your prayers. Thank you."

Someone yelled from a table in the corner by the window, "We are waiting to hear from Peter! Does he have an explanation for all this?"

"He said his explanation would be the dessert."

Everyone laughed.

"Of course I have," Peter said from behind as he stepped toward the podium, holding on to Rose's elbow. "I can certainly explain what that was all about."

There was a comatose silence in the dining hall of the Hilton Hotel, which overlooked the calm waters of the Pacific Ocean on Front Street. The sun was just setting, and one could see the magnificent shades of colors casting against the windowsill. "I've asked all of you to come this evening for a surprise announcement I have. I am grateful and thankful you have left other pressing businesses at a time like this to attend. Five years ago, I met that young lady who almost wrecked our gathering. We dated for a short while, but due to my work schedule, I was unable to make any commitments. A communication was sent via text just before the accident, saying she did not see it necessary to continue the relationship as there was no growth. The next day, breaking news was Grace Milford was killed in a car wreck that night. The police reported her car flipped and burst into flames and that she was burned beyond recognition. It was determined there was nothing left to be buried.

"Another report was Grace was thrown from the wreckage when her car flipped and burst into flames, but she was never found. It was concluded that they were in search of dental identification as that was the only evidence that could resolve the mystery. I somehow followed the link from time to time, and the CIA report would read they were still investigating. Ladies and gentlemen, please accept my apologies on behalf of my fiancée, Rose Alexander."

Peter's seemingly undisturbed mannerism brought some assurance and confidence to his guests that, at the end of his well-put-together words of deep innocence and unawareness, there was none to blame or point a finger at. "So, can we resume the evening's activity with the excitement for which we had gathered and move forward?"

At this point, a woman stood and announced herself as a longtime friend and colleague of Peter. She continued by saying how sorry she was for that outburst, and her request was for everyone to forget the confusion and continue to enjoy the ambiance. "Peter is not deserving of that type of action from anyone, but most of all, more than ever, I am requesting the prayers of all present."

Cheers were heard in agreement as the waiters served the dessert, which was strawberry banana cake, banana peanut butter chip, vanilla ice cream, and vanilla trio crispy layers served with red velvet, carrot, and pound cakes with tea or coffee. The rest of the evening went well. Rain had started again when Peter gave his vote of thanks, assuring them they would all be invited to the wedding, which would not be too far away. He gave them his blessing and pledged to stay in touch.

While everyone made their way to their vehicles, there were restaurant personnel cautioning each party to drive carefully. A few people stayed behind to speak with Peter, thanking him for such a lovely afternoon and saying that he should not be in the least worried about what happened earlier and that all would be well.

Peter and Rose held hands as they walked toward the bellboy, who gave him the keys to the Bentley. Slowly, they drove away, feeling somewhat satisfied and thanking God that it was in no way worse. Moments of silence filled the air; hearts could actually be heard pounding, and questions unsaid could be silently heard without verbalizing.

"Well, are you going to say something, Peter?" Rose softly asked in a subtle tone. "I was genuinely pleased tonight for the way you handled the whole situation. I thank you so much." She stretched her left hand toward Peter. "I love this ring so much, but I love you more." Tears of joy ran down Rose's cheek; she spoke with such sincerity and love.

Peter could not hold back the tears. He was surprised and comforted to hear Rose speak that way and that she had not picked up on talking about the disturbance of Grace Milford. Instead, she looked at the main event of the evening and the love and fellowship received from Peter and his colleagues.

Glancing over at the ring on Rose's finger, Peter broke into prayer. "Lord, I thank you for this woman you gave me under adverse circumstances. Thank you for giving me the patience to wait. You promised me whatsoever my heart desired, I should ask, and it shall be given. This is almost done, Lord. Just one more step, and I am confident that you will walk with us and direct our footsteps in Jesus's name. Amen."

It was nearly midnight when they arrived home. Peter took a rain check on stopping in due to the late hour, and he'd rather see Rose in. They kissed good night, and she watched him drive off as she closed the door.

Glancing at the table, Rose remembered the stack of mail her aunt, Stella, had brought earlier from New York. Although it was very late, she began opening a few of them. "Hmm," she mumbled. "There were quite a few from an attorney's office in New York, multiple envelopes saying the same thing with reference to my parents' estate. God has answered my prayers. I was always curious if there was anything set aside somewhere for me. After all these years, it's only now, it seems, that something had been set aside for me."

It was late; however, she began reading a few of them. She realized they were all saying the exact same thing.

Chapter 5

Dear Ms. Alexander,

We have been trying to contact you in reference to your parents' will and testament for quite some time. Would you be so kind as to send us your current email address and telephone number?

We have been trying to reach you because we are the executors of your parents' final will and testament, which came due on your twenty-first birthday. Please let us hear from you as soon as possible.

Klaus and Glasgow

Rose sat staring in amazement, wondering if this was for real or if she was dreaming. She barely slept for the rest of the morning when she noticed the time; it was almost six o'clock, just about time she should be getting dressed for work. It was still dark; the shades of night were still hanging on, hardly giving way to morning.

She decided to take five minutes just to close her eyes and reminisce. She thought of how soon she could travel to New York to see what her parents had hidden away for her. She dozed off, thinking that this would be the topic of conversation between Peter and her when he drove her to work this morning.

Her mind was still in disarray, and Rose was completely disoriented when the doorbell rang. She had no idea of the time of day. She missed a few calls from Peter, obviously, when he was on his way, but in the midst of everything, sleep got the better of her, and she did not hear the phone ringing.

"Gosh, Peter, what do I do now? I've overslept. My head feels like I'm carrying a ton of bricks. I am going to be late the second day on the job." Rose reached to the side table, grabbed her cell phone, and searched for the work number she had written on the yellow pad she had the day of the interview.

In the meantime, Peter gathered the scattered mail Rose had left all over the bed. He read those from the law firm in New York silently and then began reading out loud. Rose looked at him just as she was about to dial her office, but she felt the need to clear up a few missteps before she got on the phone.

"Peter, I had it all planned that, on my way to work, I would explain all that. I meant to tell you, but I just did not get the chance. A few days ago, my aunt, Stella, my father's sister who lived in New York, made an impromptu trip to Boca on business and thought it would be a great idea to bring along my mail that had returned due to insufficient address. They have been on her porch for many months."

As Rose began explaining the contents of the letter, Peter interrupted, "I have already read them, Rose. Oh my goodness! How much do you think this inheritance amounts to?"

"I don't know, Peter, but I will find out as soon as I speak with HR about my reason for coming in late and whether or not I will be allowed a few days off so I can take care of this urgent matter. I am a bit apprehensive about what the outcome might be. I am still excited about last night, Peter. You certainly had planned a great commitment extravaganza, I have to say. Thank you so much for loving, trusting, and believing in me. With the help of our heavenly Father, we will make a great couple."

OUT OF EVIL

The phone rang at exactly nine-thirty. Rose remembered she hadn't called HR or her supervisor as planned. "Lord, I am just a mess. I don't see how I can do this job when I have so much on my hands now," Rose said to herself.

"Hello. Oh, hello, Mr. Roberts. I am so sorry I overslept due to my surprise engagement dinner last night. I was completely blown away when I accompanied my fiancé, Peter, to what should have been a company meeting to discuss the airline he worked for, which had gone out of business. I had no idea what he had planned, and it took us to the late hour, so I overslept. I am so sorry." Rose had not planned to say all that, but the words came tumbling out of her mouth, thinking that maybe if she gave a valid excuse, the situation would be understood; after all, it was about love.

There was a bit of silence, and Peter noticed Rose looked bewildered as tears welled up. He tried to motion for her to hang up as it seemed the response was not to her liking. "Well," Peter said, "what's the matter, Rose? Is everything all right?"

Sadly, she responded, "No. That was my office. I got carried away in conversation and did not realize the time had gone, and I hadn't called. I was let go for negligence and for being irresponsible."

Peter sympathized, but the tone in his voice seemed to be a happy one. "Well, Rose, I fully agree with the final decision but not with the reasons of irresponsibility and negligence. You are far from that. Anyway, as they always say, all's well that ends well. We needed this time for so many things. Besides, there are a few very urgent calls to be made right now."

Rose composed and consoled herself, agreeing with Peter, and then picked up the phone. Deep down somewhere inside her, she breathed a sigh of relief. "This is Rose Alexander. May I be transferred to Atty. David Klaus's extension, please? Thank you."

A few minutes passed when David Klaus spoke her name. "Well, hello, Ms. Alexander. How have you been? We have almost given up all hopes of finding you. Many letters had gone out in reference to what your parents had set aside for you in the event of their demise when you turned twenty-one. It's been two years, and in spite of all the efforts to find you, we came up with nothing. Can we expect you in a few days?"

"Yes, Mr. Klaus, how about setting up an appointment for next Monday at noon?"

"Yes, of course, that would be just great. See you then." Rose excitedly hung up the phone and turned to face Peter.

"So your next call, Rose, is with the airlines. You may need a few extra days before to think things through."

"I would like for you to come with me, Peter," Rose said.

"Of course I will. I certainly would not allow you to travel alone. Furthermore, with that type of transaction, as your fiancé, I need to be there."

The hurricane alert signal brought them back to the moment. It was still the hurricane season, and most, if not all, of the radio and television stations were busy announcing the weather conditions, plus hurricane preparedness. Before making the reservation for New York, Peter suggested that they check the weather report for that day. Well, of course, somewhere in the back of their minds, they thought New York City's weather would be much better than in Boca, seeing that they were closer to the Gulf of Mexico. In any event, they made reservations with an airline departing at six in the morning, a direct flight to New York in two days. Reservations were also made at a hotel in Midtown Manhattan for a week.

The day turned out to be a progressive one as all arrangements were now in place, and this leg of it would pretty much determine the other leg of what Rose's inheritance would look like. They had at least two days to pack and be ready to leave for New York on Friday morning.

For the first time, they looked forward to spending the weekend together. Getting away at that time would do them good. There was so much to talk about and be ready for their meeting with her attorney on Monday morning.

It was Peter's choice where they would have dinner. He suggested having Italian food. Tuesday nights were never one of the busiest for dinner in the Italian neighborhoods. Rose gladly agreed as she hadn't had Italian food long before she moved to Boca. They took a quick nap and then got ready to leave for seven o'clock. Peter got into the red Bentley, which, in essence, was now Rose's. She naturally adored it but refused to drive it, at least not yet.

On the way downtown, they drove in the same direction where Peter lived. Suddenly, he remembered he had not armed the alarm at the house before he left that morning to take Rose to work. He was apprehensive about the alarm being unarmed since darkness was fast approaching. "I am making a brief stop, Rose, just to put my house alarm on. It will only take a minute."

"Sure." Rose looked at Peter with an assuring smile.

The censor light usually turned on if someone entered the front area of the house; Peter noticed that it did not come on when he approached the front door. "This is odd," he mumbled to himself. He then inserted the key but realized the door was unlocked. Peter was on high alert when he found out the door was open.

"Good grief! Did I not lock the door this morning?" he said to himself.

Unexpectedly, a voice from the living room spoke back. "Yes, you did, but the window was left open."

It was dark, and Peter could hear footsteps coming toward him as the person continued to speak. With his mouth dropped open, he managed to exclaim, "Grace Milford? What in god's name are you doing in my house?"

"Like I said, you left the window open, so I came through."

"What do you want in my house? Why are you doing this? There is nothing between us. As far as everyone knows, you have died five years ago. It's enough that you tried to destroy my engagement dinner. How dare you destroy my alarm and break into my house? I am calling the police." Peter reached for his phone but had left it in the car. He started for the door but was blocked by Grace, threatening him with Mace spray.

Rose got impatient and curious about why Peter was taking so long to set the alarm, which should only take a few minutes. Walking toward the door, she heard loud voices and detected a female voice; by then, Peter was screaming at the top of his voice in disgust and fright.

Grace was dressed in black leotards and wearing a black knitted hat. "I broke the motion light, Peter. I knew I would be seen on camera, so I broke that monitor as well. It's been a few days. I have been trying to find you. You are mine and will not marry anyone else."

"How could I be yours, Grace?" Peter implied. "I had never proposed to you in any way. We have never gotten this far, Grace. As far as I am concerned, you are dead. My God, that was five years ago. The case on you about the accident is already closed. Now, all of a sudden, out of nowhere, you appear and expect everything to be business as usual. Are you kidding me?"

By this, Rose came storming through the door, only to meet a jaw-dropping, astonishing surprise. "Is this the woman who tried to make a mess of our engagement party a few days ago, Peter?" Rose argued. "What is she doing in your house? When did you give her the keys to your house? Peter, are you insane? You came here because you knew she was here! Are you trying to make a fool out of me, Peter? What are you doing to us? I trusted you. I could never think you were in communication with this evil woman after what she tried to do to us."

"I am not in communication with this mentally deranged woman, Rose." When Peter turned around, facing Rose, it was clear to see he was livid. "Be careful of what you are saying, Rose, because you know there is no way since Saturday night I could have spoken to Grace. You, of all people, should know I have absolutely no interest whatsoever in her. If you recall, she was never mentioned as a past affair because there was nothing to talk about."

Peter walked over to his mother's old armchair and sat to take a load off. With his head buried in his hands and for the first time, he opened up, going back to as far as he could remember of Grace. "Years ago, I met Grace at a real estate event I was invited to by a friend," Peter continued. "We were both vulnerable at the time. A brief relationship developed, which lasted a few months and ended the night before I saw the news of the deadly crash. I only knew it was Grace's car because of the license plate that was still intact.

"The report was the driver was going above the speed limit. It was a rainy night. The car spun out of control, flipped, jumped the curb into a ravine, and then burst into flames. Different media gave conflicting reports about whether the occupant's body was found. Some say the driver was burned beyond recognition. Others say it was like a towering inferno as no human remains were found. Case closed.

"I am a bit disappointed, Rose, that you could ever imagine, at such an early start in our relationship, that I would try to cheat on you. We were just engaged technically a few hours ago, and since then, all I can think of is you, Rose, and putting plans for us to spend the rest of our lives together—our wedding, the honeymoon, our family business, and so on."

The broken motion light that had a separate connection with the central station triggered the system, sending signals of an intruder and also releasing the picture of the hooligan as Grace approached the house using a long wooden pole to destroy the motion light. Instead of central dispatching a call to Peter of the interruption, they sent a signal directly to the police. The instant they received the alert, four officers were dispatched to Peter's house. They drove quietly around the bend, approaching the house without using the siren.

What a rude awakening it was when, to Grace's surprise, all four officers walked through the front door with guns drawn. One of the officers looked at Grace and asked, "Why are you here? Is it you who did this? Aren't you the same person who disturbed Mr. Swazi's engagement party a few days ago? You were given a warning never to be seen anywhere close to him or his fiancée."

Grace was now in serious trouble with both the law and Peter. She was arrested for breaking and entering and was handcuffed and shoved inside the police car. The officer read her rights as she sobbed hysterically.

Peter was asked if he wanted to press charges. "Not at this time, Officers. With the humongous amount of work I have lined up concerning my mother's business, I am in no way interested in adding anything to it. Plus, in a few days, I will be accompanying my fiancée to New York to help her take care of her parents' business. I just need clarification that the next instance of any type of violation of my privacy from Grace will result in incarceration."

The officers drove away, taking Grace to detain her just for the night with a second warning. In the meantime, she was told she was responsible for the damages done at Peter's house that needed to be repaired immediately.

The mood for dinner went flat. Rose was waiting in the car for the officers to leave, wondering to herself, *Now what?*

Of course, the air was dry, and it felt as though the rug was pulled from under them. Peter opened the door of the Bentley and was met with sobs coming from Rose. He got inside the car but said nothing.

His cell phone rang, breaking the ice as he sat at the wheel. It was the police calling to inform him of the many guidelines laid out that Grace should follow, including giving her an ultimatum, to which she quickly agreed: never to go anywhere near Peter, his fiancée, or his property. Peter was also told she would be leaving anyway for Europe to assume a new position with the airlines within the next few weeks.

"We would like to make arrangements for tomorrow morning to have the technician replace the units, Mr. Swazi, if that's all right with you."

"Sure, it will be all right, about ten o'clock?"

"Yes, I will be there."

"Seems we have to forget dinner, Peter. It's quite late, and maybe most of the restaurants are closed," Rose muttered.

"Well, let's see if there might be something closer. The food obviously will not be as delicious, but at least we won't die of hunger."

There was a bit of calm as Peter drove around the block, remembering an old Irish restaurant he had not been to in a long time. The owners knew him quite well from a child growing up; his mom would sometimes have takeaway when she did not have the urge to cook. "How do you know they were open or that they were still there, seeing it was such a long time ago, Peter? Rose asked.

"It's family-owned. They are always handing down the business from one generation to the next. I can always depend on them over the years."

It was ten o'clock when Peter pulled up on the cobblestone pavement in front of Ben's Eat-In and Takeout, and sure enough, they were open and still serving dinner. Peter walked in with his usual jolly self and was greeted by a waitress who had been there for quite some time and remembered him as a kid. "Hey, fella, long time no see. How have you been?" she asked. "I was at your mom's funeral the other day—my condolences. You were a bit busy, so I didn't bother to interrupt. We missed her. She was a good woman, a hard worker in Saint Paul's, and one of my best customers." She grinned, and then she showed them to the table.

Peter pulled the chair out and invited Rose to sit as the waitress went for the menu. Soup and salad was the final entrée offered for the night since it was just before closing, which was great at that hour anyway. As they both waited to be served, Peter reached across the table and held Rose's hands.

"Well, young lady, I am not beating a dead horse, but that was some scare tonight. I want you to understand I would never ever do anything to hurt or make you uncomfortable. I have not the foggiest idea how all that went down, but I am asking you to please never question my actions or think I would in any way cheat on you. I love you with all my heart. You have changed my world, which was so drab and gloomy. You have given me hope by the grace of God. Without you, I have no idea what would have happened to me, from the accident of my mother to her death and burial. Your warmth and your godly demeanor help me wake up each morning hopeful, encouraged, and with you on my mind. I spend my day praying for you. I knew you were mine from the minute I laid eyes on you and offered you shelter under my umbrella that day of the storm.

"You have to trust me, Rose. You have to believe all that I'm saying to you. God made you for me because no one else could fill this void. This place, I know, is reserved for God, and next is just for you."

Rose guessed that it was their cooling-off period; they were too tense not to break. They were both snorting all over their faces. They just had to let it out. The waitress served them and offered napkins for them to clean up. There were no words spoken by Rose; she was a royal mess. Peter had to actually force her to have at least the soup.

It must have been about an hour when they noticed it was closing time. Peter asked for the check when Maggie, the waitress, told him it was on the house. They both thanked her profusely and held hands as they walked out the door.

Rose was not fully composed when they got to the car; the tears rolled down her cheeks again. Peter held her close in an embrace and tenderly caressed her hair as he muttered soothing words of endearment. "Everything is okay, Rose. Sometimes in one's life, things have to happen to bring out the assurance we so often need."

Within a half hour, they were home; it was already late. Rose offered that Peter stay the night since the alarm on the house was broken anyway, which might not be safe. "You can use the guest room. It's across the hall. Let me just turn the bed down and bring fresh towels and sleepwear with new toiletries."

"I'm surprised you had all these in place, Rose. Seems somebody is getting ready for a new life."

With a half smile, Rose thanked Peter; they kissed good night and then went to bed. The next day was the only day they both had to pack for New York with so much to do in so little time.

"Good morning, gorgeous. You look amazing. I hope you had a good night's sleep. Now, what I am asking you is to please forget about yesterday. Yesterday is all behind us, understood?"

Rose nodded and headed to the kitchen to make coffee.

Peter then went back to his room to get dressed as he had to leave to do his packing. They had no time to sit over coffee and doughnuts. Peter took his cup, kissed Rose on the forehead, and then headed out the door. "I will call you as soon as the technical crew gets done with the sensor and alarm, and I am packed, okay?"

Afterward, Rose sat for a minute and reminisced on last night's drama but refused to be a victim of it. *First, so that I don't forget*, she told herself, *all important papers, letters, identification, and any other papers that will be required for the meeting on Monday, I'll need to have them ready and packed.* There was a whole lot of reasoning as she gathered the necessary documents.

It was now two o'clock in the morning. Rose's packing was completed. Their flight leaves at six. The arrangement was Peter would pick Rose up at four thirty and then head to the airport, where he planned to park for the weekend. The airport was only thirty minutes away. The alarm was set for her to be up at three-thirty, which gave her enough time to check on Peter, making sure he was up and ready as he was a slow dresser.

Everything worked well in going to the airport; they were on time, and the flight was a great one. Peter walked off the aircraft, making sure he held Rose's hand, reassuring her that he would always be at her side. She had not been to New York for close to a year and had always mentioned how much she hated flying and airports. That was why it had taken her a while to decide whether to move to Boca.

They collected their luggage and headed outside to the black SUV that was already waiting, compliments of the hotel, with the driver holding their name cards. "My goodness, such service!" Rose said to Peter, settling in with a comforting smile.

"Thank you so much. I certainly appreciate the effort of my fiancé," she said with a chuckle.

Chapter 6

The streets of New York on a Friday evening were busy as usual—the hustle and bustle of yellow cabs, buses, bicycle riders, pedestrians, and peddlers on almost every corner, trying to catch a last-minute sale here and there. The borough buses whizzed along, with the subway riders dashing across the streets and down the escalators, hoping to get on the next train, which could be heard rumbling in the far distance. The smell of roasted cashew nuts had Rose's mouth watering. "That used to be my pacifier on weekends. Oh, I missed so much of the city life," said Rose.

The car took a little longer than anticipated because of the usual heavy and snarled traffic. "Wow!" Peter exclaimed, trying to absorb every detail of a buzzing city life. "All this excitement makes me dizzy."

They arrived at the Hilton Hotel, and the bellboy took their bags while they checked in. Peter had asked that their room be reserved as they would be arriving early before the usual check-in time and would be tired. Their room was the penthouse suite overlooking the Hudson River, with a beautiful sunrise outlining a silvery blue skyline. For the next two hours, they welcomed the best sleep in a long time.

It was now noon, and yes, they were hungry. It was a great idea for them to have room service. The kitchen had stopped serving breakfast since eleven, but they could make them breakfast as a special treat.

Saturday morning posed a completely different atmosphere in midtown; Peter suggested they should go for a walk for a few minutes so he may familiarize himself with the big city. Rose couldn't even recall the last time she was here. She knew she had to make a connection a few times, passing through Kennedy Airport, but her brain couldn't focus now to know when exactly. Rose listened intently with a questioning expression.

"In another couple of weeks, you will be right back flying again, Peter. We need to talk because there is so much yet to be done. It's as though we haven't begun."

"We need to put some things into perspective as soon as this meeting is over tomorrow, Rose. Hopefully, we don't have to be coming back for any reason. What time is your appointment on Monday?" Peter asked.

"Twelve o'clock," Rose responded.

"Okay, we will have enough time for breakfast and to be on time."

"Let's talk about the details and plans, Peter," Rose interjected, "after dinner. How about an early one?"

Peter welcomed the idea as he was beginning to feel famished. There were quite a number of restaurants along the strip as they walked. "Anyone will do," Rose suggested.

"All right, let's go here."

"Tavern on the Green, I've heard this name so many times before."

"Yes, this is a famous place where a lot of actors and actresses and those of the upper echelon of society dine."

It was an exceptionally warm afternoon with only one outdoor table for two remaining. The waiter, a stately tall gentleman with a slight Trinidadian accent, led them around the chocolate fountain and past the beautiful patch of hydrangeas and sunflowers into an area of several diners under a blue and burgundy canopy. He showed them to their seats.

Rose's cell phone rang just as they settled down to place their order; it was her aunt, just checking to see how everything was as she hadn't spoken to Rose for a few days. "We are fine, but Aunt Stella, we have just sat down for dinner."

"What do you mean *we*? Who are you referring to?" she questioned Rose.

"Oh, we need to talk, but this I will say quickly. I am now engaged to be married. I met someone some months ago. I'm in love, Aunt Stella. God has provided me a handsome airline pilot who loves the Lord first, but I will fill you in as soon as I get back."

"What do you mean as soon as you get back? Where are you?"

"I am in New York, Aunt Stella. I had to quickly make arrangements. When I went through the letters you brought me a few days ago, there were some very important information and documents included that required my immediate attention. There were a few deadlines I've missed because my letters were with you all this while. Come to think of it, you could have mailed them to me. You have my correct address. Why didn't you?"

"To be honest, Rose, I thought most of them were junk mail of just someone advertising their new law firm. It had not dawned on me that they were letters of importance. What are the contents?"

"It has to do with my parents' will and testament," Rose answered. "I had no idea that my parents had set aside anything in their estate for me once I turned twenty-one. I am meeting with Klaus and Glasgow at twelve o'clock tomorrow morning."

Aunt Stella became vociferous. "You cannot go about this type of business with a stranger, Rose. I need you to cancel that appointment now and wait until I am able to go with you. After all, I am your aunt and only living relative. I will be home next week, and then we will go together."

"No, Aunt Stella, I will not cancel my appointment. Sorry, you have been getting my mail all these months since I left New York, and not once has it ever dawned on you to communicate with me or even send them to me. Well, I am twenty-three years old, old enough to make my own decisions. Furthermore, Peter is not a stranger. My attorney says it would be okay to have him with me. If I need you for anything tomorrow, I will certainly give you a call. I have to go, Aunt Stella. Dinner is served. I will call you tomorrow when I am done."

Peter admired the way Rose handled the situation. He kept nodding in approval, commending her for her tenacity during the conversation.

The two settled down to a sumptuous meal that they did enjoy, and they had already decided they would return on Monday after leaving the law office. "This visit is a short one, Rose. We need to look into when we can return to explore more of New York."

Peter and Rose arrived at Klaus and Glasgow on Monday morning at eleven fifty-five. After registering at the concierge, they were met in the lobby and escorted to the office. A tall white-haired gentleman came over with a warm smile and stretched his hand to shake Rose's hand but immediately withdrew; instead, he gave her a hug. "My name is David Klaus. You will meet my associate, Charles Glasgow, in a few minutes. So, you are Peter?" he asked and motioned for them to sit while he took a seat behind his old mahogany desk.

"I am delighted to meet you both. Congratulations on your engagement. I wish you both the very best. Well, young lady, we have almost given up hope of contacting you. My secretary has tried so many times to get in touch with you, if I am not mistaken, even before you moved away. What took you so long? We had no forwarding address, no telephone number, or email address. Nevertheless, I was glad when we spoke last week. And by the way, you can call me David."

He reached over, picking up an old file that looked like it had not been used often for many years. David opened the folder and started pulling out forms that were already written up, which Rose saw at a glance and read, "Last will and testament." He handed them to her to go over and sign.

At this point, Peter pulled his chair close to hers so they both could read together. However, they were just reading words, but nothing registered. And in all that excitement, it was as though nothing made sense.

In the meantime, David Klaus continued to sign other documents they needed. That was when Charles Glasgow, his partner, walked in. They briefly acquainted themselves as they both went over all the necessary steps to close out the long-awaited lofty inheritance.

This could have been a very long process, but they were the executors, and there was nothing premature about this transaction. The rest had to be done when Rose got there. There was quite a bit of paperwork for her to sign. Her parents were executives at Black Pearl Associates, a large hedge fund group on Wall Street, for over twenty years and had quite a bit of stocks and bonds, 401(k)s, and multiple bank accounts. Her father had Rose as his sole beneficiary. She was only a child, of course, and for sure, they were not expecting that anything would happen to them at such an early age.

As Rose glanced through the folder, she saw pictures of them, which she feared she would see. Her heart broke; she began sobbing like a little girl. Peter offered her a glass of water as he tried his best to console her. The lawyer averted his eyes for a moment in an understanding gesture of Rose's vulnerability. It did not take her long to regain her composure as she looked forward to the closing of the meeting.

The transition went well; everything was self-explanatory, and all transfers, fees, and taxes were done. There were no claims filed. All the necessary tax returns were taken care of with the internal revenue. They had obtained the release forms stating Klaus and Glasgow transferred all balances electronically to her bank account for immediate deposit. Rose signed the closing receipt, which stated the receipt of her inheritance.

Rose was not obligated to come back to New York for any reason. David assured her that if there were any loose ends, it could be taken care of via email or phone. "It's our delight to have you coming in, Rose. We are excited to know that everything went well. The closing statements will be filed with the probate court as soon as possible, just to inform them that all obligations have been taken care of."

They shook hands with Peter and again congratulated them on their engagement with the assurance that everything would be fine. "I will make sure to invite you to the wedding," Rose said with a grin. "You are on the guest list already."

David accompanied them to the door, wishing them all the best in their future endeavors and saying that if they ever needed anything or were experiencing any form of difficulty, they should not hesitate to let him know. The strange part of the transaction was David never mentioned what her parents had left Rose. He simply acted like she already knew, and then, adding to the mystery, she did not ask.

Anxiously, Rose asked Peter, "What are the contents of the inheritance? Is it anything of substance like yours?" she said it factitiously.

The yellow cabs were already lined up outside, so they got into the next available one. It was then Rose said to Peter, "I can hardly wait to get to our hotel room, where we can comfortably scrutinize all this paperwork. It all happened so fast that there was barely any room for questions. All I know is they were doing the right thing."

They were so mesmerized with what had just transpired, as well as engrossed in their own world, that they did not realize they were at their hotel until the taxi driver said, "Here we are, the Hilton." He handed them his card and suggested that if they needed to do any sightseeing or any additional business around the city, he would be happy to assist them.

The moment they walked into the lobby, Rose's cell phone rang. It was the attorney, David Klaus. "What's the matter? Did I forget something? Is everything all right?" Rose spoke hastily ahead of him.

"Everything is okay, Rose. It's your aunt. She just arrived here at my office and wants to dispute the closing out of your parents' last will and testament. She presented a completely different will from the one I did with your parents, saying that's the latest."

"What?" exclaimed Rose. "Is she out of her mind? Is she still there?"

"No. I had to have security escort her out as she began to be loud. She threatened to sue the company, saying we falsely acquired documents, and she is sure they are not legitimate. But don't worry, Rose, your parents have legitimately had us write their will and testament, and we had everything filed in the probate court for years already.

"Your aunt was never included, and even if she felt your parents were indebted to her, a time was given for her to file her claim with the courts. It's been years now, and we have not gotten any notifications about any claims, not from her or from any other attorney."

"How did she obtain the will she has?" Rose desperately wanted to find out. "Did you look it over?"

"I glanced over it quickly and saw where she would be awarded quite a bit."

"Quite a bit, like, how much?"

"Like three million dollars, plus the house in which your parents had lived."

"Oh, is that so? I will call you tomorrow sometime, David. We've just arrived at the hotel." Out of ignorance, Rose asked David, "Do you think, by any chance, she is included, but we overlooked her?"

"Oh no, Rose, I would have pointed that out to you in the letter we sent you. And also, she would have been summonsed to the closing. From what I gather, Rose, she got those papers under false pretenses. There is nothing said by your parents in your inheritance that includes your aunt. You are your parents' sole beneficiary. It's all yours—their life insurance policies, all their estates, bank accounts, stocks, and bonds. You'll see it. Have you noticed how well the transaction went, Ms. Alexander? From the day your parents made that will, nothing has changed. That was the best thing they could have done for you twenty years ago. We carefully administered everything, Rose. I would hate to know she got some gigolo attorney to falsify a will and testament to suit her own ego. She would be in a lot of trouble."

"We will talk tomorrow, David. Thanks for the information."

Now I understand why she got so upset when I told her I was in New York to take care of my parents' estate. That explains it all. I am most disappointed in her actions. She thought, all this while, she was the sole beneficiary, maybe waiting to see the post from the government of unclaimed monies or real estate for any living relative to claim. Well, I would have been the first anyway if that was the case. I am the one and only child. Well, well!

Stella Alexander was the only sister of Mark Alexander. After the tragic loss, the courts agreed that she could raise Rose like her own daughter. This she did to the best of her ability; she grew in want of nothing. The cost of her education was taken care of.

Peter and his fiancée had room service that night as they needed to satisfy their hunger and anxiety, where this inheritance was concerned with a good meal. While eating, Rose looked over at Peter curiously. They opened the large brown manila envelope, and there it was—the unthinkable, the unimaginable, and the unbelievable. "Oh my God." Rose was blessed beyond her wildest dream. Enclosed was also the key to her parents' safety deposit box at Barclays Bank midtown. That was why it was all so easy—the money transfers, real estate transfers, stocks, and bonds, to name a few.

They both held each other in tears and prayer. "What the enemy meant for evil, God turned it around." Although it all happened under tragic circumstances, the blessings of the Lord overtook too young lives and set them in a place of abundance, a place of wealth beyond what they could have ever imagined or conceived. All this time, Rose thought she had to struggle to build a life of comfort all on her own. Little did she know that God had an unending wealth in this life, ready and waiting for her. His blessings are in abundance, and it adds no sorrow.

"Thank God," Peter whispered, "yes, with all this."

They spontaneously sang, "Thanks, thanks, I give you thanks for all you've done. I am so blessed. My soul is at rest. O Lord, I give you thanks."

After all was said and done, they never got a call from Aunt Stella. The next day, Rose spoke to David. He had gone ahead in calling the attorney who drafted the will presented by her aunt. They recognized the names of the attorneys who made up the bogus paperwork, but sadly, they were both deceased, and there were no copies filed with the firm.

"The good thing, Rose, is that the signatures she has of your parents are not a match. You see, Rose, after the sudden death of your parents, your aunt Stella thought they had not made a last will and testament. Maybe she thought they were too young to think about a beneficiary, so she went ahead and assumed nothing was done. That is a crime committed, Ms. Alexander. It's a felony. She had those lawyers draft a will and have them backdate the paperwork one year before, claiming all that monies should go to her because she was your father's only sister."

"Why then didn't she claim everything after my parents died? I really noticed she barely mentioned them, and to be honest, I thought she cared and did not want to remind me of the tragedy. I knew she was hiding something."

"Rose, just for your information, one copy of the original last will and testament with a key is here at Klaus and Glasgow, another copy and key is locked in the safety-deposit vault at Barclays Bank in midtown, and we gave you the third set. This she has no idea of.

Therefore, there is nothing she could do. The will she has is null and void."

Because of time restraint on Rose's part, Klaus and Glasgow had gone ahead and alerted Barclays Bank that Rose would be visiting them to retrieve the items from her father's safety deposit box but would contact them upon her arrival in New York.

"Well, Rose," Peter said, yawning and stretching his long muscular arms, "let's see if your aunt will try to contact you after everything has been exposed. She should be ashamed of herself. Are you thinking of having her arrested, Rose?"

"No," Rose replied. "After all, she took the place of my mother. She stepped in and took full responsibility of raising me to be who I am today. I will speak to her, though I certainly will not allow that behavior of hers to go without redress. She is a good person. I will try to get her back on track. I have also forgiven her deeds already. Many times, the enemy preys on the innocent and unassuming and blinds their eyes, especially with the love of money, which the Bible says is the root of all evil. Aunt Stella allowed the enemy to get the better of her."

"Some folks would go to the extreme and beyond scruples and common decency to collect what's not theirs."

"When the dust settles, I will compensate her. I will show gratitude and gratefulness for all she has done for me, but in the meantime, my prayer will be for her to seek the Lord while He may be found and to call on Him while He is near. It does not hurt to save a soul, Peter. Let's try to show her love and forgiveness. Now I know why she hadn't opened my mail. She really thought those were junk advertisements. After all, there were so many. And, of course, she had not a clue her brother had made a will before his death. Wow, that's a shame."

Peter's inheritance was a much different business venture. His mom sensibly did her will in the presence of her attorney, her pastor, and the church's secretary. She then gave it to Reverend Hurling in the event of her death. From the get-go, the house and all her bank accounts were in both their names, and Peter was the sole beneficiary. All Peter needed was his mom's death certificate along with his identification, and everything would be exclusively his. Peter's mom lived like a miser; in all the years after everything was turned over to her in her accounts, she had not once made any type of withdrawal. Aside from the initial dollar amount, the interest accrued was a lot. Peter had more than he could spend in a lifetime.

In another couple of days, Peter and Rose would be back in Boca Raton with a lot on their plate to take care of. It really would not be possible for Rose to commit to a nine-to-five job and do all that needed to be done at this time.

It had been two days since Rose signed on her parents' inheritance, and still, she had not heard from her aunt, Stella. She would call when she was good and ready. *Maybe she is just a bit scared because she was caught in a terrible scheme.*

Chapter 7

While packing for their flight the next morning to Boca Raton, Peter's cell rang; it was Raymond Castro, his old boss. He has recommended him to the CEO of a new company that might be looking for experienced pilots. Peter did not hesitate in his response. "Raymond, I am considering a leave of absence from the Air Force at this time. It may not be permanent, but at least for a while. I am now in New York with my fiancée. We are getting back tomorrow and will be in full planning mode for our wedding. Sorry, Raymond, but I will have to turn this offer down. Thanks anyway for your thoughtful recommendation. Please email me your address, Raymond. The wedding will be soon, and I would love to have you. We have not yet decided exactly when, but we will be making a decision as soon as we are home tomorrow. I have a strong feeling, though, it may be just before the Christmas holidays."

"All right, Peter," Raymond responded. "Let me know the date as soon as you have decided. I am so sorry you are not accepting the job offer at this time. I recommended you highly, you know, but I understand. So if ever you change your mind, please send me an email. Bye, for now, Peter. I'll wait to hear from you."

Rose felt a bit hungry, and as soon as Peter finished with his call, she asked him, "Do you mind us eating in tonight?"

"Sure, I don't mind. Order whatever you like, and I do think you need to call now before it's too late. It's too hot to be outside anyway. Plus, we have to be at the airport at the latest seven o'clock to be on time for the eight-fifteen flight to Boca."

The telephone on the nightstand rang. Rose answered as Peter stood in front of the bathroom mirror, putting on shaving lotion. The call was from the receptionist at the lobby's front desk. "Ms. Alexander?"

"Yes, this is she. How may I help you?"

"This is Monica at the front desk. There is someone here to see you, and she wants to come up. It's a bit late for visitors, but she insisted. Is it okay to send her up, or can you just speak with her? Her name is Stella Alexander. Is she a relative of yours?"

"Yes, she is my aunt, but let me speak to her if you don't mind. Thank you."

"Hello, Rose, this is Aunt Stella. I need to speak to you before tomorrow. I know you have plans to leave in the morning, but can you postpone leaving until we can have a family meeting? There are a few very important family matters I would like to straighten out as soon as possible."

Rose listened until she was through talking. "Aunt Stella, how are you? I figured you were doing well. I wondered if you were still in Boca as I never heard from you for a few days. And what you tried to do after the closing of my parents' last will and testament surprises me. I am not a child, Aunt Stella, and you knew there were some things I needed to know, but you kept them a secret. Why? Now you just show up this hour of the night, seriously asking me to cancel my flight for tomorrow. No, I will not be able to do that, Aunt Stella. We have pressing business to take care of. Therefore, that's not possible. You have my number. Why didn't you call instead of coming? I told you if I needed you for anything, you would be the first to know. I had no reason to call you, Aunt Stella. All went well, as expected. So you came all the way across town for nothing."

Aunt Stella listened without saying a word.

"Are you there?"

"Yes, I am here," she answered.

"We will be having dinner in a few minutes. Care to join us?"

"No, Rose, I have already eaten."

"Well then, if you care to wait in the lobby until we are done, then I will come down, not for a meeting but just to see you."

"No, Rose, it's late, as you have rightly said. I will have them bring my car around and will call you tomorrow after you are home. Sorry for all the misunderstanding, but I can explain. Have a good evening, and enjoy your dinner." Aunt Stella got off the phone without giving her regards to Peter; she did not even acknowledge the fact that her niece was not alone but was with her fiancé. She sent a clear signal that she was not interested in knowing who this Peter was or where he came from. Rose had mentioned to Aunt Stella that Peter was coming to New York with her and going to be there during the signing of the paperwork on her inheritance. Stella opposed strongly, saying he was a stranger. Little did she know who Peter was and what his worth was.

Dinner was delicious, just simple chicken fingers with french fries, baked beans, and a side salad. They had ordered a small bottle of red wine to serve as the nightcap. Peter rang the front desk, asking for a wake-up call at six o'clock, and also inquired what time the shuttle left for the airport. They needed to be up and ready and be in the lobby by six-thirty as the shuttle left then. There were additional pickups before getting to the airport; it was a short trip anyway.

They arrived before seven o'clock and thought it best to have breakfast. A few of the kiosks were opened with not much of a choice; most of what they had were prepackaged sandwiches. They were happy to have them anyway; at least that would suffice until they got home.

They talked all the way home; it was weird and wonderful when they were told to fasten their seat belts and put away their tray tables as they prepared for landing. It felt as if they had just boarded. The conversation was productive as it took the monotony and the trepidation of flying away, making it a relaxing and interesting flight. Peter was happy that they had a great trip and that everything went very well. They were elated to be home; it felt as though they were gone for weeks.

They took the shuttle to the car park, which was not far; Peter encouraged Rose to drive just to see how well she did. Of course, trying to convince her did not work. Her challenge was she had never driven on the highway; as a matter of fact, ever since she received her driver's license, she had never driven.

Rose never had the luxury of a car. She was encouraged to learn how to drive after college, hoping she would someday be in possession of her own vehicle. Most of her friends were given cars as graduation gifts from their wealthy parents, but she had no interest in owning one. After she obtained her license, there was never a pressing need for a car.

When Peter gave her the red Bentley, she was virtually at a loss for words; she could not believe he seriously gave it to her. Now, driving it was another issue. He tried to convince her. "It's okay, Peter," was Rose's response. "When I feel confident with a few refresher courses and get my mind ready, then I will drive and give it a try."

It was twelve-fifteen when they pulled up in front of 2 Saint Paul's Place. They sat in the car for quite some time, trying to decide what the rest of the day should look like. Peter decided he would help Rose unpack and get settled in, and then they would both go to his house and do the same. Rose liked that idea very much as they made a pledge that, as much as possible, neither of them would be apart for any length of time.

Just before they got out of the car, Peter held Rose's hand as they thanked God prayerfully for taking them to New York safely, allowing them to execute the business at hand, and taking them home in one piece. Everything seemed in order when Rose entered the house, but something felt a bit weird by just observing.

"What is it, Rose? Is there something wrong?" Of course, Peter was not as observant as Rose, and he was not as familiar as Rose was with the layout.

"Maybe it's in my mind, Peter, but I could almost swear I had packed up the rest of the mail Aunt Stella gave me after I had taken out those I needed with me to New York and left the rest in this drawer. Why are they strewn out on the kitchen table and opened as if they were read?"

"Maybe you left them there and thought you had put them away, Rose."

Rose sat down, looking quite uncomfortable and agitated. "I know that's not my style, Peter. I have never done that, and even if I were home, the mail would be put away in that letter holder I have mounted on the wall. There was someone in my house, Peter, and I have a strange feeling that Aunt Stella was here."

"How could she get in, Rose? Have you given her keys? Are you listening to yourself and what you are saying, Rose?" The minute Peter mentioned *keys*, Rose rushed to the front door. With much curiosity and anticipation, she lifted the welcome mat, hoping the spare keys were still the way she taped them to its back. Sure enough, the keys were there, but the tape had come loose.

"Rose, I am freaking out," Peter said.

According to Rose, Aunt Stella spoke with her on Sunday and discovered she had gone to New York to claim the inheritance her parents left her, and Rose refused to cancel her attorney's appointment to suit Aunt Stella's convenience. Aunt Stella seemingly took a cab to Rose's house as she had not the faintest idea who the attorneys were or where in New York they were located. Evidence showed Peter that she had gone through every drawer in the house until she found the mail she had brought from New York.

"I can tell she searched through in a hurry until she found the information she wanted as I had not taken all the letters with me. In my observation, she had a car waiting. She forgot to return the mail to where she had taken it. Thank God she locked the door. It seemed she horridly threw the key back under the mat and left on a flight to New York to try to sabotage the process."

"Do you really believe she is capable of doing all that meandering, Rose? Why would Aunt Stella do such a thing? This is breaking and entering into your house. It's a serious charge, Rose."

"She had no other way of finding where the attorney's offices are if she had not done this, Peter. She realizes it was not junk mail she brought me. Klaus and Glasgow—she probably remembered seeing it on the outside of the envelopes. There were so many letters from them. When she handed me the mail, she mentioned she believed they were all junk mail in a sarcastic way. It wasn't funny. I guess she realized, after all, they were not. Stella Alexander went through all that to stop the process of me claiming the inheritance."

"That was not a nice thing for her to do. I believe she did all that she could for me with a motive. She believes there is something hidden that she is the only one entitled to have. From what I can remember, Peter, while trying to make the reservation for New York, there was only one early morning flight on Monday. I decided against it as it was more convenient for us to leave on Friday so we could get some extra relaxation in and be ready for Monday. Her flight arrived at ten thirty. But by the time she cleared the airport to get to my attorney's office, we would be long gone. It seemed she skillfully went past security up to the attorney's office. David mentioned she rushed into his office about an hour after we had left."

"She is unbelievable."

They spent the rest of the afternoon at Rose's place, with the decision they would not think about Aunt Stella and what she may have tried. Rose had already decided she would compensate her for the years she served as a mother after she lost hers. Rose's inheritance was a done deal that could not be reversed, case closed.

"How could I miss Aunt Stella's insatiable appetite for wealth? Maybe it's because I was focusing on her goodness, raising me as her own child. It was only now since this entire legacy was given to me that I observed her greed. The blessings that God gives a person cannot be reversed. What He does is done. Even through adverse circumstances, if He allows certain things to happen for His people to be blessed, then so be it. We are not going to accentuate the negative but stay focused on the positive."

It wasn't much for Peter to unpack; they were done within fifteen minutes and had time to take a break and freshen up. Peter mentioned that dinner would be at one of his favorite restaurants, located on the outskirts of Boca. "It is called The Cliff. I will leave the rest as a surprise," he said with a touch of confidence. "You will see when we get there."

As usual, dining, movies, and other means of entertainment and whatever they occupied themselves with each evening were left up to Peter as Rose was still not altogether familiar with the community. She had not had the time to move about as she would love to. Right away, Peter read her mind and made a promise that he would take her on a sightseeing trip soon. "I really do think I need to familiarize myself with Boca if, indeed, this is where we intend to settle down and obviously start a family."

While driving, Rose suggested they call Father Hurling's secretary to make an appointment to meet with him about counseling before marriage and to get his expertise as an experienced pastor and marriage officer. "We need guidance and prayer before we get settled on a date for the wedding." Peter agreed and thought that was a wonderful idea. Father Hurling's secretary could not be reached at the time of their call; it seemed office hours had passed. However, they were able to leave a message.

They were finally on their way to dinner, tired and starved. For the most part of the day, all they had were the sandwiches from the kiosks at the airport. "Here we are," Peter said with a chuckle, having to drive around a few times looking for a suitable place to park. The parking lot was overflowing, but they noticed there were other cars parked in the grassy area.

It was usually crowded this time of the year. The summer months had the most people dining out. From the appearance of the outside, it seemed as though there was some sort of merriment going on. They saw balloons with unusual decorations, starting from the entrance and going all the way inside.

It was a beautiful evening for the location of this restaurant; it was built on the edge of a cliff, overlooking the ocean, with the dominance of the setting sun casting an unusual silver lining behind the clouds. This magnificence was always something to look forward to. It became a tourist attraction, making the ambiance somewhat romantic with a feel of nature.

Hundreds of couples came from all over the world yearly just to enjoy the scenery as they sat beneath the skylike roof, where the stars could be seen. "This is the famous Cliff." Peter ended his description, turning to Rose as they hugged for a while.

There were two ushers standing at the entrance, welcoming the guests as they walked in. Rose verbalized, "We did not make reservations, Peter."

"Oh," he replied, "there's no need to ever make reservations. The good thing about The Cliff is that there is always room, no matter what they are having. There are quite a few rooms that provide the same ambiance, and no one is robbed of anything."

Attendants were busy and efficiently seating everyone as they came in; they were taken to a small round table right by a window overlooking the deep end of the cliff. It was only noticeable if one had to look over and down at the ocean. "What a fantastic view!" Rose smiled and said, "It is absolutely breathtaking."

The drink menus were already placed on the table for their convenience, although there was a bar. They were treated especially well as it seemed their slightest orders were their commands.

There was a live band playing well-known instrumental music, which was great entertainment for the evening. Peter and Rose were a little apprehensive as they wondered if they were intruding on a special occasion. A few of the waiters were busy attending to each table, taking the drink orders, and placing a red rose when they were done. Just then, someone spoke over a microphone.

"May we have your attention, please?"

Everyone was in their own conversation, laughing and talking, some just enjoying their drink and having a curious look.

"Welcome to The Cliff. Beginning tonight, the management and staff have decided to do something special in thanking our regular guests, tourists, and visitors for your unwavering support of The Cliff over the years. We will continue to do this on a random night selected by management once a month during the summer."

The MC continued by saying, "I am seeing the questions on your facial expressions as if to say, 'What?' Also, in addition to everyone receiving their favorite drink on the house, we have an extra-special, pleasant surprise for a lucky couple at the completion of this evening's dining. We have decorated our restaurant to depict a festive occasion, all geared toward giving back to our faithful diners and encouraging those who are just getting to know us."

The entrée was an enjoyable one. Almost everyone made several trips, replenishing their plates and giving a nod of satisfaction.

The MC asked that they all remain seated until everyone had eaten just so no one would miss the chance of becoming the lucky couple who would receive the pleasant surprise. Peter and Rose looked at each other with a shrug as if to say, *Is this for real?* They did not give the prospect of winning any thought. The servers brought out Frozen Haute Chocolate ice cream sundae, which seemed to be a favorite of everyone. It was enjoyable to the last drop.

There was a noticeable change in the tone of the music, which put them on alert. They were planning something differently. The MC made the announcement that the time had come to bring on this special surprise. He continued, "We need each couple to search your table. The prize is hidden somewhere beneath the surface of the table. At the count of three, you will begin the search."

Pandemonium broke out as all the couples searched in suspense, hoping they would be the winner. Peter hesitated to begin his search. Rose thought it was preposterous. Undauntedly, they joined in, and in a few seconds of search, Peter pulled out a business-card-sized note that read, "If you are married, your next anniversary celebration will be fully paid for by The Cliff. If you are planning your wedding, the entire wedding reception will be paid for by The Cliff."

Abruptly, Peter jumped up with such a thrill, beaming with joy and happiness. "I found it!" he exclaimed.

The master of ceremonies came running over to congratulate them on their lucky win. Peter and Rose were asked to join the managing staff at the podium. It was as though this was the grand finale of the night.

The second couple winning the anniversary celebration also screamed from the far left and bolted toward the podium with their winning ticket, jumping and waving it in the air. They did not wait to be asked to come to the managers at the podium. With all that excitement, they just ran over anyway.

The winning couples were asked when the dates of their wedding and anniversary would be; with bated breath, Peter tried to explain the few months they had been engaged and that they came to have dinner to discuss the soonest possible date for the wedding and where the ceremony would be held. The anniversary couple was able to document their date right then and there.

Chapter 8

It was a jackpot night for both couples; it was as though the whole shebang was planned with them in mind. Peter and Rose could not begin to fathom their good fortune all around. In a couple of days, they would be able to inform the management team at The Cliff of the date of their wedding. As fate would have it, they were right in line for their surprise event and ended up winning the big prize.

"Not that we could not afford a wedding of our own," Peter said, looking pointedly at Rose. "God knows we can, but I believe if we weren't to win this prize, we would have never gone there, in that place at that time. We will take all the blessings God has to offer us."

"Just think about it, Peter. There were so many restaurants all around, but we were led to The Cliff in particular. I call that divine leading." They exchanged information with Mrs. Brady, the manager for the Cliff, and assured her they would have a wedding date for them in a few days.

It was eleven o'clock when the band began playing the usual goodnight tune. Getting to the end, one could see the regular attendees saying their so-long to friends and acquaintances. Peter whispered to Rose, "I think we better get going also. We have quite a drive ahead of us."

Walking toward the exit, they were bombarded by some of the guests offering their congratulations and all the best in their future endeavors, some wishing them God's choicest blessings with their wedding plans and hoping jokingly they would be on the guest list. There was an elderly gentleman sitting with his wife near the exit door; as they approached the door, he got up and walked pompously toward them. *Obviously*, Rose thought, *he knew Peter.*

"Peter," he said with a broad smile, "how are you?"

"Fine, thank you, sir. Please remind me. Have we met?"

"No, we haven't. My name is Ben Scott, and I am one of the owners of the Bentley car sales and rentals. You rented from us and then bought the Bentley afterward for this lovely fiancée of yours. Congratulations. You deserve to win this prize. You are a good man. I've heard so much about you from my colleagues in the Air Force." Ben kept talking. "So, how is the Bentley running?"

"Oh, it's running fine, Mr. Scott. It's the best I have ever driven, but my fiancée is scared to drive as she is not energetic about driving yet."

"Really? I understand. Well, come down to the business later in the week. I might have something more comfortable for her." Ben did not give Peter a chance to respond; he tapped him on his shoulder and said, "Good night. Drive safely. Just give me a call when you are on your way." He waved them good night and sat back down to join his wife.

Peter and Rose went through the door with a feeling of ecstasy; things were just turning around in their favor. "God is a good God. He promises us the 'blessing would overtake us by the way,' but we did not understand that is what He meant."

When they got to the car, they had to sit for a while, trying to grasp all that just took place. "It's been one blessing after another. The claim on my parents' will, the finished transaction of your mother's will, the buying of my Bentley. It was a joy to see how happy we both are. The fatigue we felt earlier suddenly disappeared. I feel like a contented purring fiancée right now," Rose said with a smile. "What do you think, Peter? Mr. Scott didn't bother to ask you if you could afford a second car."

"I'd like to know what he is insinuating," Peter responded. "I have not the least idea, but I believe God. For some reason, Rose, this happiness certainly helps take away the sadness of losing my mom, the sad remembrances of your parents, the awful disturbances with Grace, the cheating with Aunt Stella, the loss of my job, along with anything else at this point I may not be able to recall. We have every reason to thank God."

Peter's phone had been on vibrate since the event, and he had not noticed a missed call from Father Hurling's secretary. However, a message was left with an appointment for Wednesday at ten-fifteen. "That's a good day to start with our wedding plans, in the morning when we meet. I suggest we first look into a few favorable dates. We can have semblances of organization and not convene on Wednesday without bringing something to the table. Let's talk tomorrow, Rose. It's much too late, and I need to catch up on a bit of news before I actually get to bed. I think I need to be at my house tonight."

"I don't think it's a wise idea anymore for either of us to be alone in our houses, Peter. Remember our pledge? Why don't you stay the night? Then, in the morning, we'll both ride over to your house."

Peter was a bit strong-willed; however, Rose managed to persuade him to occupy the guest room as usual. It was magical to see how they complemented each other with willpower and class; it was decided between them both that they would not be sexually involved until the night of their honeymoon. They decided to focus on getting to know each other well—likes, dislikes, moods, and expectations. They had become inseparable, providing companionship for each other with the understanding that they would be married in a few months, and the assurance was "till death do us part." Therefore, the limits of their exploring each other were clearly understood. They were anticipating many years of holding, loving, trusting, and being there for each other in every sense of what marriage was all about, as they intended to spend the rest of their lives together.

They both were still full from all that they had eaten at The Cliff. They had no room for their regular cup of tea or coffee. After embracing, though, they prayed a short prayer and hurried off to their bedrooms.

Tuesday's sun came beaming through the gigantic picture window, followed by the sound of the seven o'clock train as it went barreling down the track. The train tracks were about half a mile behind Rose's house at Saint Paul's Place, with the train station just a few miles ahead. The speed and ferocity with which it passed made it sound as though the tracks were coming apart.

As the train began pulling into the station, a call came from Aunt Stella. She took the train to Deerfield Beach Station, which was about three miles away. "Hello, Rose, it's Aunt Stella. My train is just pulling into the Deerfield Station. I will need a ride to your house."

"Are you kidding, Aunt Stella? What do you mean you need a ride to my house? What were you thinking, leaving New York, coming all this way without notifying me in advance? You broke into my house on your way to New York without my permission and ravaged through my things, looking for something you have no entitlement to. I could have had you arrested, Aunt Stella. You are behaving like you have all rights. When I moved here almost a year ago, I heard nothing from you. Now, suddenly, you are usurping authority over me and my privacy? I am not pleased with your behavior, Aunt Stella, with all due respect. I love you. You know that, but you have gone just about too far."

"Well, Rose, you left New York yesterday. We hadn't had a chance to get together to discuss any of our business."

"What business? There is no business for us to discuss, Aunt Stella. You seemed to want to bully your way into something that does not concern you. You went to my attorney with fraudulent papers, trying to lay claim to my inheritance, and you have been chasing after me ever since I told you I was going to New York to settle my business. Aunt Stella, I am not in a position to accommodate you at this time. For the next few days, my fiancé and I will be busy trying to get our wedding plans underway."

Peter heard Rose's voice across the room and thought it strange that she would be so audible first thing in the morning. He snuck across and began eavesdropping. After hearing enough rambling, he reckoned it was Aunt Stella. He then knocked on Rose's door and asked if he could speak with her. Rose hesitantly gave Peter the phone, unbeknownst to Aunt Stella, who was in the middle of trying to make a convincing statement. Before she concluded, Peter interrupted her.

"Aunt Stella, this is Peter Swazi, Rose's fiancé. I have been aware of all your undertakings. Don't get the wrong impression. I'm appreciative of all you have done for Rose, according to what I was told. Ever since the death of her parents, you cared for her like her own mother. Rose has no intention of turning her back on you, especially now, but you need to understand she is no longer under your jurisdiction, and it's disheartening to know you got on a train from New York to Boca with not even an iota of communication. Not good.

"Here's my suggestion. Inquire about the nearest hotel that will accommodate you for a few days. On Friday, when we have fulfilled our pressing appointments, I promise you we will have some time to sit and discuss 'business.' Agreed?"

"Okay, Mr. Swazi, I will see about that. Thank you."

"Good morning, my darling," said Rose as she looked up at Peter, who was now standing over her.

"Good morning to the love of my life. I trust you had a good night's rest?" Peter inquired.

"Yes, I did, until the sound of that speeding train woke me. Let's get dressed and get out of here. We can have coffee at your house."

Preparing to leave the house, Rose asked if she could drive a part of the way.

"Of course. Do you think you can handle it?" Peter asked.

"I'll try. Let's just see." Nervously, Rose got behind the wheel. With a frightening jerk, she tried to move off.

Peter got rather concerned; it seemed it'd been too long since Rose had driven. "I tell you what, Rose," he said with a slight smile. "I will arrange to have you do some refresher classes to get you in shape for the road."

Rose agreed immediately, got out, and walked around to sit in the passenger seat.

It was twenty minutes to Peter's house without traffic; with traffic, it was close to a half hour. They got there within that time as the work traffic had already gone. When Peter got in, he first got the teapot, cups, and saucers and began making coffee. There was a lot to think and talk about over breakfast. "What are we having for breakfast?" Peter yelled out.

Rose was entering the house with her computer and calendar.

"On second thought, let me run up to the corner where there's a Dunkin' Donuts. I'll just grab a few." Peter hurried away and, in a short while, returned with an assortment of doughnuts.

They sat down for a quiet breakfast. The first thing on the agenda was getting a date for their wedding. They had a few dates swirling around in their heads. They were thinking if they should get married on Thanksgiving weekend, Christmas Eve, or the first Saturday of the new year. They wanted a time when everyone was busy with their own festivity so that the list would not be too long. The reason was they were considerate of The Cliff's gift to them and did not want to overdo the guest list.

"I think we should have a Christmas Eve wedding, Rose, when we ring in the festivity."

"I am sold on that, Peter, December 24 at two o'clock. That was easy enough. After our meeting with Father Hurling, provided that date will be okay, we can send out the invitations."

They spent the rest of the afternoon quietly planning their future home, trying to decide where they would live. Then, one of the startling things they decided was that they would not reside in either of their homes. Peter suggested they contact a realtor to see if there were any homes for sale in any of the more affluent neighborhoods, gated if possible. They would prefer to build a new home, but time was of the essence.

A wave of contentment wafted over Rose, and she looked at Peter with tender, loving eyes and upturned lips for a quick kiss as she wrapped her arms around his neck. "At least we accomplished a lot in just one afternoon," she said softly. "Our ten-fifteen meeting with Father Hurling will give us the green light to move forward."

Eating out that night was not thought of. Peter and Rose had been quite occupied for the past few days, getting their business squared away. "Let's order from Cannoli Kitchen. Their Italian food is to die for," Peter suggested. "And their delivery time is quite reasonable. If we order now, I'd say in another half hour, they would be here."

They ordered an Italian dinner—carbonara with cheesy Italian bread. Peter had already gotten in his winery Moscato, which was always a welcoming wine that was good for any occasion. The order was called in, and they were guaranteed a quick delivery. Indeed, it took a little less than a half hour when the doorbell rang. Peter was busy preparing the dining table with a couple of his mother's bone china. He even added candles to complete a romantic setting. Rose offered her help, but he refused.

His mom had an old gramophone that played LP records and was still in good working order. Peter found one of his favorite LPs by Frank

Sinatra, "Come Fly with Me." This song described dream vacation spots and honeymoon locations. *Wow, he is doing it*, Rose thought.

With all that fanfare in order, they settled down to a beautiful night of a scrumptious Italian dinner, dancing to "Come Fly with Me" playing over and over. "Where do you wish for us to go for our honeymoon, Rose?" Peter asked.

And without any hesitation, Rose girlishly yelled out, "Dubai!"

"Okay, you will have your desire. Dubai is the place."

They were done with dinner at nine o'clock, and Peter started packing his overnight bag. There was no reason for them to be up very late as they had to be on time for their appointment with Father Hurling in the morning.

It rained heavily overnight, which was obvious; they did hear the raindrops. "If we were at my house, Peter, we would have heard it making music on the roof. I am always thankful that their experiment worked well."

Peter was intrigued as he listened. "If we ever built our home, Rose, I would have to have those contractors install a roof like yours. How beautiful that must have been," he said with a jovial grin.

Walking toward the Bentley, they noticed little tributaries here and there in succession, running toward the lake at the other end of the highway. There were also a few fallen trees blocking parts of the roads, but they managed to maneuver their way around them. They arrived at Saint Paul's Cathedral quite safely in spite of the many hurdles. Father Hurling was already standing on the church's porch, waiting for them. He was concerned about them weathering the heavy winds and rain, with a strong possibility of a cancellation.

They were invited into Father Hurling's office, and right away, his secretary offered them coffee. Although they had just had breakfast, they politely accepted as they got underway with the needed discussion. "So what can I do for you, Peter? How are you getting along since the death of your mom?" Father Hurling asked.

"I am doing fine, Father. Of course, I am missing her more and more every day, but God has sent someone to me in a strange way, and that's my reason for wanting to talk with you this morning."

Father Hurling pulled himself back in his big armchair and took his glasses off with raised eyebrows and a wide grin. Then he said, "I'm listening."

Peter continued by introducing Rose Alexander as his fiancée and then went into the long story of how they met and what happened that stormy night when his mother was injured and eventually succumbed to her injuries.

"Quite interesting," said Father Hurling. "I remember seeing Rose at your mom's funeral but thought she was a family friend."

"We got engaged some months ago and are asking if you could do us the honor of joining us in holy matrimony on December 24."

Father Hurling reached across, picked the telephone up, and buzzed his secretary to come in with the calendar of the year's events. "You know that's a very busy day for a wedding," he said to Peter with a giggle. "What time would you do this, son?" He said it with a fatherly voice.

"We are requesting a two o'clock ceremony if that time is available."

Just then, the secretary knocked and entered with the yearly calendar. Father Hurling looked over his appointments and asked, "Do you mind changing to an earlier time? I already have committed myself to a previous engagement for the time you request."

"What's the next available time, Father?" he asked, taking a quick glance at Rose.

"How about one o'clock?"

"That's fine with us, sir."

"You know we need to have a few counseling sessions before the day, though, with both of you," said Father Hurling. "Let's get those dates on the calendar right away." His secretary, along with Peter and

Rose, was able to pencil in the two available counseling sessions they would need before the wedding.

Peter reached into his jacket pocket, took out an envelope, and handed it to Father Hurling. He sat back with a lump in his throat and said to his pastor, "Do you recall the day of Mom's funeral, you handed me an envelope without saying a word?"

"Of course I did. How could I forget? So what is this?" Father Hurling asked.

"After reading the contents, I see Mom asked you to keep it in case she transitioned. Well, this is a part of what she asked me to do. I would like to thank you, sir, for the way you took care of my mother, along with the parishioners and staff from the children's orphanage. Therefore, she saw it fit, if she passed, to make this donation on her behalf."

Peter broke down a bit as he made his speech; Rose held his hand, assuring him he would be just fine. Peter was already standing when he was joined by Father Hurling. Taking his Bible, he opened it to Psalm 91:10–11 (KJV):

There shall no evil befall thee,

neither shall an plague come nigh thy dwelling.

For He shall give His angels charge over thee,

to keep in all thy ways.

Father Hurling asked that they join hands with him in prayer as he delivered them into the hands of God the Father. He asked God for complete protection from the devices of the enemy as he went about like a roaring lion, seeking whom he would devour. Father Hurling thanked Peter on behalf of the church for the generous gift his mother had donated to Saint Paul's Cathedral and promised to spend it wisely. He assured them there would be no honorarium for his services as he considered them to be family.

When they drove off, Rose said, "Darling, it's as though a great weight has rolled off my shoulders."

Peter asked, "Why?"

"I felt as if that date for our wedding would be an impossible one. Christmas Eve?" She cried and thanked God for her answered prayer.

Through her tears, she remembered arriving in Boca after settling down. It was one of the first places she visited, Saint Paul's Cathedral. On her scheduled evening walks, the eye-catching, picturesque landscaping forced her to enter the sanctuary. She told Peter of the evening before they met, recounting in detail her time spent in the cathedral. It was the church he knew quite well; on his days off, he would visit it with his mom as often as he came. He knew that the grandeur of it truly gave the feeling of being on a sightseeing tour.

Rose recalled herself saying, "If I would ever be a bride, I would love to have the pleasure of walking down the center aisle of this church on my wedding day."

"Little did I know the reality of it is almost here. On December 24, I will pledge my troth to the man of my dreams—yes, to you, Peter Swazi, to be my wedded husband, to be faithful, to love, and to be committed. You are the love of my life, Peter. We met under strange circumstances, and here we are, planning a lifetime together."

Rose took Peter's hand in hers and thanked God for what He was doing and would continue to do. She prayed a prayer of unity with much love and thanked God for a man of like faith, dignity, and honesty.

Before Peter realized it, he began making his promises; one would think this was the wedding vows. He promised to love her in pain and in laughter, in wealth and in want. Then he looked at Rose outlandishly. "I had never heard you speak that way, Rose. I am at a loss for words. You took my breath away. Thank you so much, and by the grace of God, this marriage will be that of a different nature."

They had no clue in which direction they were driving; it was as if the thought of everything falling into place overwhelmed them somewhat. They had all intention to visit the nearby card store to purchase a few wedding magazines and also the invitations to be sent out. "Let's swing around, Rose, to the card store I had in mind at first. We might as well initiate our plans by getting the list together so we can send the invitations out as soon as possible."

"We can't rely on having Friday for ourselves, bearing in mind that we promised to have a consultation with Aunt Stella then."

The card store was only ten minutes away. When they got there, they were almost at closing. However, they were permitted to browse for the last five minutes but surprisingly got what they exactly wanted.

On the way home, Peter's cell rang. "Hello… yes, this is he. How may I help?"

"It's Ben, Ben Scott from the Bentley rental. Remember we spoke last weekend when I insinuated that you get your fiancée a car she could handle? I thought you were taking me up on my offer."

"Yes, I am," Peter answered.

"So when are you coming here?"

For a moment, Peter went quiet. "I am awfully sorry I haven't gotten back to you, Ben. Can we come tomorrow in the late afternoon? We have a prior arrangement, but I promised we will be done in time to stop by."

Ben was happy to know they would be able to come.

They were home by midafternoon. When Peter opened the door, he stumbled on a note pushed under the door addressed to Rose. It was from Aunt Stella. Rose apprehensively opened it. "What is it now?" Peter anxiously waited.

The note read,

Dear Rose, I am sorry I will not be able to meet with you both tomorrow. In my haste, I totally forgot I had an important doctor's appointment I had scheduled for a long time, which I was advised not to miss. I will leave on an eight o'clock flight tonight back to New York and thought we may have this discussion some other time. Please forgive me for disrupting your schedule. Sorry, I'm not able to fulfill the appointment. I will speak with you soon after my appointment.

They stared at each other, feeling somewhat remorseful. "Something isn't going well with her, Rose. I am detecting an underlying problem."

"Let's wait to hear from her. I would say after tomorrow."

It wasn't necessary to ring Ben just to inform him of the change. "We could certainly use the morning to start working on our wedding invitation list."

There was quite a bit of leftover from dinner last night. While Rose prepared it, Peter grabbed a quick shower and then continued setting up as Rose did the same.

Chapter 9

They were settling down for dinner when Peter stared out the kitchen window that opened into the garage. "What is it? You are acting as though you've seen a ghost, Peter."

"Well, it better be a ghost because I just thought I saw someone looking in at us. And when my eyes caught her, she hid behind the car."

"Gosh! We had left the garage door open."

"Let's go out there. Whoever it is will have to explain to us why they are staring through our window."

"Okay, we will see. I have my baseball bat in case there is trouble."

They both went through a hidden door to the garage, but there was no one there. "I know I saw someone, and for some unknown reason, she looked like Grace Milford."

"Not her again, Peter. I thought she was warned not to be seen anywhere near us. This time, someone is in serious trouble. Let's go around the side gate, Peter. There is a car parked there. I could see it from my bathroom window. I really did not pay much attention as I thought it was my neighbor's son home from college."

"Well, let's see."

As soon as they were within reach of the motor vehicle, it sped away, but Rose was able to get hold of the license plate.

"I will ask Ben tomorrow when we get there to put a trace on it."

"That's a good idea," Rose suggested.

They were a bit nervous, not knowing the identity of the person. "What if it's not Grace Milford?" They got back inside, immediately closed the windows and doors, and then activated the monitoring system.

After dinner, they were able to start the list. In a few minutes, they were counting eighty-five people; most of them were friends of Peter. "I can't forget my friend Abigail and her husband. I made sure to list them along with a few of my immediate neighbors."

Ben had sent a text message suggesting they had a lunch meeting when they got there. So they had a light breakfast of toast and scrambled eggs, which were good enough with their favorite Maxwell House coffee.

By midmorning, the list was completed, and they were ready to meet Ben. It was roughly an hour's drive, according to the GPS. Sure enough, they were there by twelve-thirty.

They met first over lunch at The Farmer's Table downtown. They were seated under some gigantic umbrellas, where they were safely shielded from the heat of the sun and also in case it rained. It was just a short walk from the Bentley car lease and rentals, but what they noticed was there were adjoining car dealerships displaying several emblem signs like BMW, Lexus, Volvo, and Corvette, seemingly owned by the Bentley dealers also. They made a mental note of how vast a business Ben owned.

They totally enjoyed sweet potato fries with a mixture of chicken wings and stuffed crabs, washed down with homemade icy lemonade. The entire ostensible humbleness of lunch made it rich and tasty. Ben certainly did not try to impress them with anything more elaborate, and he knew they would have been satisfied with that lunch setting and menu.

Just before they were through with lunch, Ben palpably directed his question to Rose. "So, Rose, you are not careful to drive the Bentley, eh?" He had a silly grin.

"No, Ben," Rose responded. "That's not my type of car."

"Okay, let's walk back to the office."

The walk was just a stone's throw. While they walked, Ben made a quick call and spoke softly to someone they presumed to be his car sales department. By the time they got to the steps leading to his office, a uniformed sales representative drove around a spanking new white BMW. He pulled Peter aside and whispered in his ear something Rose could not hear. She saw Peter smiling from ear to ear as they both walked toward the BMW.

In a few moments, Rose was asked to analyze it and to let him know her thoughts. "So what do you think, Rose? Do you think you could handle this car?"

She stuttered to respond, but she clearly wanted to make sure she didn't embarrass Peter or herself. Then she audaciously responded, "Yes, Ben, I think this is a better choice for me."

"Congratulations, Rose. Please accept this as a pre-wedding gift from my wife and me. At the surprise dinner last weekend when you won the wedding reception gala at The Cliff, your husband mentioned you were not comfortable driving the Bentley. It was then we both decided we would do something special for you. This is in advance of your big day. You should be able to get around doing chores in case Peter, at times, would not be able to drive you. Also, since you are a bit rusty around the wheel, we have arranged with one of the driving instructors from our school to give you a refresher course.

"And to you, young man"—he turned to Peter—"you cannot be left out, the groom in waiting," he said with an infectious smile. "We are aware that your job went into chapter 11 at a time when everyone needs finances. I had known your mother for quite a long time. I am sure you haven't any knowledge of this. She was such a great friend of my wife, Sheila. It would take me the rest of the afternoon to put in plain words the closeness of their friendship, but all that is not necessary at this time. We loved her unconditionally. We were not able to attend the funeral due to circumstances beyond our control. I willfully did not bother to mention any of this when we met at The Cliff."

Ben took an envelope from his coat pocket and handed it to Peter. "Take this. It's for you both to enjoy. It's an all-expense paid honeymoon to Dubai. It's open for you to make the necessary reservations."

Rose could not hide the tears as they rolled down her cheeks. Peter fought to keep his away. They did not know how to thank Ben. "These are unbelievable gifts. God's blessings are unexplainable," Peter managed to say.

Ben had transferred all the appropriate papers already in Rose's name. The car was licensed and insured for the first two years. "Oh my goodness, this is astonishing and humbling at the same time," she said.

"Forgive me. I must return to work." Ben shook hands with both of them and asked one of his sales representatives to deliver the car later that Friday and to make arrangements with Rose for a convenient time for delivery.

They had already gotten in the car when, suddenly, Peter remembered he needed to have Ben inquire into the license plate number Rose took from the car that was parked outside the house the night before. Peter quickly ran in with the information. "Ben." Peter popped his head in the office. "I need to ask you a favor. There was a car with this license plate." He handed Ben the number. "It was parked outside our house last night. We saw a strange woman looking through our kitchen window and heard noises. We cautiously went out and began looking around to see who it was when the car sped off."

Ben took a quick look at the license number and recognized it to be one of his rentals, and he quickly brought the information up on his computer. "What?" Ben had a surprised look in his eyes. "Why would she be outside your house?"

"Who is she?" Peter asked.

"Her name is Grace Milford. She rented from us last week. She should have returned the car a few days ago, but we have not seen or heard from her. We were just getting ready to notify the authorities."

Peter was flabbergasted, and his consternation quickly turned into annoyance.

"Do you know her, Peter?"

Before Peter could answer, he rushed out and got Rose to return to the office, where she would be safe. He had not trusted the likes of Grace. Rose was frightened and upset. This was sheer coincidence.

"What was she doing at your house, Peter?" Ben asked.

It was then Peter was forced to explain to Ben the whole ugly story of Grace Milford and how they had a short affair but thought she had died in a car accident about five years ago. "Our friendship had not grown into anything of substance. We broke off for communal reasons. The relationship just was not going anywhere. After my engagement with Rose, I had an announcement dinner. Grace showed up, which was a shocking surprise to me and my guests. She almost ruined the night. She also broke into my house, attacking me and demanding I not marry anyone else but her.

"The sheriff was called, Grace was arrested, and I was assured she would not ever come near me or my house again. Also, I was told she showed proof of her relocation to another country. They made her sign an agreement and held her to her word, and then she was let go. I am totally at a loss to see her showing up at our house again in the manner she did. I have no idea what she could possibly want from me now," Peter said out loud with a fatigued look.

"I am convinced that some people are created to cause you grief, and that becomes their sole purpose on the earth," he continued. "For five years, she was presumed dead. I had no intention of proposing then and even now. It's worse. We were just beginning to get acquainted with each other. No bonding happened."

In the middle of the discussion, Grace drove in at the car return entrance. Ben thought it a good idea to summon the police. The station was literally across the street. The sheriff, to whom Ben spoke, arrived promptly and was just in time to see Grace Milford delivering the rental car and trying to rush off in a waiting vehicle at the top of the street.

"Hello, Ms. Milford, not so fast. Do you remember me? I am Sheriff Thomas Wakefield. I thought we had an arrangement the last time I was called to an incident caused by you at a Matt Court Road address. An order of protection was filed against you, and you stated to the judge that you would be relocating to another country. What are you doing here? Furthermore, why were you at Rose Alexander's house last evening? Can you explain the reason you are trying the same scenario again when you are aware of the consequences explained to you in my office?"

Grace responded, "I thought I would stop by last night to say goodbye to Peter and to wish him all the best in his future endeavors. I did not feel I should leave for Europe in the morning without saying goodbye. See, these are my travel documents." Grace handed them to Sheriff Wakefield. "I am booked to leave on British Airways at ten o'clock tomorrow night."

"I will only allow you to leave," Sheriff Wakefield interjected, "if I can confirm you on British Airways for tomorrow night. Why don't you call to reconfirm your flight and let me speak to the airline representative?"

Grace hesitated.

"What's the problem?" Sheriff Wakefield asked.

"My phone battery died. I will not be able to make the call."

"Well, let me call. I can use my phone. May I have the number, please?"

Grace hadn't shown any signs of retrieving the number or even made an effort to find it. The boarding passes she showed the sheriff looked legitimate, but they were all phony; she bluffed him because she thought he would just believe the story of her departure to Europe and release her.

In all this, Ben was transfixed. This was another time he found himself at a loss for words; he was sort of lost in the middle of this conundrum. He thought he was just notifying the sheriff of this guest who rented from them and overstayed the time limit of the car rental, and here was Peter with a license plate number that matched their ownership. Also, she was caught breaking and entering someone's home using their vehicle for a repulsive crime getaway. Peter explained to him what the entire collusion was all about. Ben had no idea who Grace Milford was other than just a client who rented one of his cars.

Sheriff Wakefield radioed an arresting officer who read Grace her rights and took her across to the precinct. She was found carrying a loaded, unlicensed revolver, along with different types of knives and duct tape, as well as a large blanket in what looked like a carry-on travel bag. A canister of Mace was also found in her pocketbook. A full container of gasoline was found in the trunk of the car she returned. She was also charged with invasion of privacy, along with breaking and entering.

It seemed her plans for Friday night were thwarted, and in her haste to return the overdue car that afternoon, she completely overlooked the container of gasoline she had in the trunk. Grace was determined dangerous and a flight risk by the prosecutor and was refused bail. Trial and sentencing were set for three months from then.

Sheriff Wakefield kept Peter informed of the progress of the case and suggested that both he and Rose should be prepared to be witnesses if it came to that. He also suggested what he believed Grace's intentions were. "I know this might not sound like you are out of harm's way, Mr. Swazi, but you are. There is nothing for you to worry about. This time, I can assure you she will be put away for a long time. From our investigation, this is the type of lifestyle she has lived. She's been involved in a range of unlawful activities and somehow cunningly got away with it. She is also wanted in Boca for armed robbery. Seems that's the way she supports her existence. Friday nights are always a night that most people dine out and then go to a movie after. Therefore, she does her looting then, attacking the innocent and unassuming. This is totally unacceptable with the indelible law in Boca and an unbending decision to make her pay for her misconduct."

Peter and Rose were both deadbeat from the various undertakings that day. They both decided not to discuss what happened but just dismiss the whole conundrum. There was so much to be done now that the wedding date was set for December 24.

"Let's just order in and then spend the rest of the night getting these invitations ready for mailing." That was a deal between them both. They did not mind eating again from Cannoli Kitchen, seeing they really had the knack for making some great, delicious, and tasty dishes.

It was getting a bit late when Rose realized she had not heard from Aunt Stella. "Let me call to see if she is doing okay."

The phone rang for quite some time before it was answered by a strange voice, clearly not Aunt Stella or anyone she knew. Politely, Rose asked to speak with Ms. Alexander. "I am sorry she is not available at this time. May I take a message?" Rose was asked.

"Could you have her return my call? This is her niece, Rose Alexander, calling from Boca Raton."

"I am not sure she will be able to return the call for a few days. She was admitted to the hospital yesterday. Her doctor needs to evaluate her to determine some findings."

"What hospital is she in?" Rose asked.

"She is in New York-Presbyterian in Lower Manhattan. I will text you the number so you can speak with her doctor. He will be better able to assist in reference to her condition."

Peter answered the door as the restaurant delivered their order for dinner.

"You know what, Peter, let's not discuss Aunt Stella over dinner. We will eat and do the invitations. Then tomorrow we will talk about it. It's not that serious. I do believe it can wait."

Dinner was awesome as usual, and of course, Peter complained of eating too much. Now, they were in no mood to sit to write invitations. Rose made a great suggestion. "Why don't we ask the card store manager, Betty, if they will be able to do the invitations for us for whatever it costs? It's just tiring after a full day to sit and handwrite eighty-five invites."

The idea was such a great one that Peter did not hesitate to agree. "Let's retire for the night. Then we will deal with this in the morning after breakfast."

"You know, Peter, on second thought, there is a very good movie on television tonight. It's an old one, but I am sure we will enjoy it. I am sure it's already begun, but for what it's worth, let's tune in."

"Yes, of course. *The Godfather* has been one of my favorite movies for many years now. It does not matter how many times I've viewed it. I am never too exhausted to watch it over and over again."

They watched until it was two in the morning. Rose must have drifted off to sleep with her head cradled on Peter's lap. He gently shook her by the shoulders. "Your bedtime has passed, young lady. Let's go." They kissed good night, and they each stumbled into their bedrooms. Before Rose's head hit the pillow, she was out like a light bulb.

The pleasant aroma of freshly brewed coffee wafted into her room simultaneously with the brilliant, intense sunlight coming through her bedroom window. Peter did not have to summon her for breakfast. By the time he started toward her bedroom door, Rose was already sitting at the table.

She sat there and just savored the moment. It was a perfect setting—Peter with the coffee pot in his hand, the table nicely laid out with freshly cut flowers in a vase. It was such a gracious invitation for breakfast. It was like a breath of fresh air ever since Peter and Rose met. Her life had been rearranged in such a magnificent way that she could not explain. She was cognizant of the fact that they met under unusual circumstances; theirs was a fairy tale. Not every day would you get to meet the love of your life, the one who was tailor-made for you, a person of faith and substance.

God is everywhere. He is omniscient, ubiquitous, and the one who decides the path to our destiny. Rose had learned to trust God and to understand Him. If we have a relationship with God, He will have one with us in return.

In contemplating her move to Boca Raton, Rose spoke with the Infinite One. She asked Him for direction and guidance into a strange place, and He directed her divinely. *Yes,* her thoughts swooned, and she found herself in another realm when she first sat for breakfast. She was in deep communication with her inner being. *It is an ecstatic feeling to know that you have someone in your life whom you can connect with spiritually, a soul mate who knows what you are thinking before you even verbalize it. Peter connected with my musings and began praying, asking God for instruction, protection, and assistance, but most of all, for Him to be our planning committee.*

Breakfast was quiet, cheerful, and filled with the love of God and love for each other. They agreed on most decisions without any hidden agenda. They had no secrets; everything was transparent as crystal, and that added to the oneness they were experiencing.

It was ten o'clock; by this time, the card store was open when they arrived. The manager agreed to do the invitations and see to it they were mailed out. Betty Cohen also suggested that Peter and

Rose order the floral arrangements for the bridal party as a package, and then there would not be any additional cost for them to do the invitations.

"Of course," Peter and Rose answered in unison. "We would only need the bridal arrangement, one for the maid of honor and two boutonnieres for the best man and the groom. It's a small bridal party."

Betty documented the order on the calendar without a problem with a reminder of the time they needed to have them delivered. It would be a busy time. Therefore, it was beneficial to have all this in place early.

Chapter 10

Leaving the card store, Rose suggested they ask her friend Abigail Suarez to be her maid of honor, and Peter would ask Ben Scott to do the honors of being his best man. They immediately phoned Abigail and Ben to ask if it was possible for them to do this favor of standing in as witnesses on their wedding day on December 24.

"Does this mean we are invited?" Ben jokingly responded.

"Of course, it would be my pleasure." Peter could not help but chuckle at his humor. "An invitation is in the mail, Ben, for both of you to attend."

Abigail was also hilarious upon knowing she would be a part of her friend's wedding in such a festive season. "I will be busy, you know, Rose, but will set aside that afternoon for you. Please send me the details."

"It's in the mail," Rose responded.

"God is in control," Peter said as he looked at his fiancée smiling. "I am glad everything is just falling into place. The hurdles we have got to overcome are living proof that God favors our union and that He is a waymaker because He always makes a way for us. Mom's song says, *'Got any rivers you think are uncrossable? Got any mountain you can't tunnel through? God specializes in things thought impossible, and He will do what no other power can do.'*"[5]

5   Oscar C. Eliason. "Got Any Rivers." 1931.

Wedding plans were now well underway, yet there was quite a way to go and quite a bit more to do. They needed to call the travel agency to make final plans for their Dubai honeymoon trip and to make sure all that was secured. Again, they thanked Ben so much for his unbelievable gift to them.

In the middle of Peter's imagination running wild, he realized that he had turned on an unfamiliar street. There were mansionlike Tudor houses with sprawling manicured lawns and acres of land between neighboring houses. "Let's turn on the GPS," Rose suggested. "I detest the thought of being lost."

Siri said, "In two hundred feet, make a left turn."

As they turned left, there was a sign posted on a gigantic lawn surrounding a mansion-like house that read, "House for sale by owner," with a phone number to call. Rose saved the number to her cell phone.

Before she could put the phone back in her purse, it rang. It was Aunt Stella calling from the hospital. Rose had not gotten the chance all morning to speak with Peter about the conversation last evening about Aunt Stella being in the hospital. "Hello, Aunt Stella, how are you? I waited to hear from you yesterday after your doctor's visit. I became a bit worried about not getting your call. Therefore, I took the liberty to call, and someone answered your cell and informed me you were in the hospital. Please tell me what happened."

"The doctors told me, after quite a few tests, I have stage 4 Alzheimer's. It's bad, Rose. I can't do anything on my own. I have been in denial, but it has caught up with me. I can't even remember where I was yesterday. My memory is like the waves of the ocean.

"I need your help, Rose, when I am discharged from the hospital. Someone will be moving in to help me. I need you to make sure she is someone trustworthy. My trip to Boca a few days ago was mainly to let you know my suspicions about the feeling I am having. I know I have made some terrible mistakes. I am asking for your forgiveness."

"I don't hold grudges, Aunt Stella. You are my father's sister, and I cannot forget how you took care of me after their passing. I have a gift for you. When I am able to visit you, I will bring it."

"I don't need a gift at this point in my life, Rose. Whatever you're preparing to compensate me, please use it for yourself. Like I said before, I made some horrible mistakes for whatever reason I am not even able to rationalize. I was a cohort in forging documents with regard to your inheritance that almost landed me in prison. I apologize, and I am deeply sorry. Whatever I have had been sufficient. Also, just for your information, my bank accounts are also in your name. Therefore, whatever the end is, please use it wisely. Do you think you would be able to move back to New York to take care of me until my final days, Rose?"

All this happened while Peter kept looking at Rose and eavesdropping, trying so hard to hear as much as he could of Aunt Stella's dilemmas.

"Aunt Stella, I will not be able to move back to New York, and you know that. I am settled here with plans underway for our wedding. I will arrange to see you soon."

Looking back at Aunt Stella's behavioral pattern, Rose realized this must be the onset of Alzheimer's that was affecting her all this while unbeknownst to her, but she herself could not diagnose. Rose did not see this coming; she was fully aware of Aunt Stella's irrationality at times but had no idea of her debilitating condition until it now had taken serious effect. "I will arrange for someone to be there with you, Aunt Stella. You will not be alone. Don't worry. My prayers are with you."

"Thanks, Rose. I will see you soon." She then hung up.

Peter was anxious to hear about the entire conversation, including the call from the night before. Rose had to apply a lot of patience, repeating the whole scenario to Peter. "It's just one thing after another, Rose. It seems there is no end to it. As soon as one thing is resolved, here comes another."

"I know, Peter, but all this puzzle will soon be resolved."

Peter had an incredulous look; he just thought that Aunt Stella was a wiseacre.

"She is really sick, Peter. Remember you had mentioned a while ago that you think something is wrong with her?"

"Yes, you are right, I did mention that. Rose, I think we better brace ourselves for the inevitable."

Without realizing it, they were pulling into the driveway. Peter recalled the house for sale that had such an impressive landscape. "Let's call the number you jotted down. I remember the address is 11 Haven Court."

"Do you think we can afford that house? Looks like it's going for an arm and a leg—I mean, the asking price must be way above our means."

Peter threw his arm around Rose's shoulder. "I do believe we can afford whatever the asking price is. Between the two of us, we can have whatever our hearts desire." He said this with such assurance, accompanied by a kiss.

"Oh, Peter, I am not used to having lots of money. I have forgotten all about my inheritance, maybe because my affections are on things above and not on this earth." With a comforting smile, Rose remarked, "It really helps, though, to know that you have the means to live comfortably." She reached into the refrigerator for a cool drink. "Want one, hon?"

"Yes, I could use a cold drink too myself. Thank you." Peter decided he would go ahead and make the call himself for what it was worth. "Looks like that house is going to be our dream home, Rose. I am picturing us getting it ready and moving in before the night of our wedding. I have such a good feeling about this."

He made the call. "Hello, my name is Peter Swazi. I was driving through your neighborhood today and saw this house with a For Sale sign. Do you mind advising me about how I can go about getting some information on it? My fiancée and I are about to be married, and our sights are on that lovely house. I notice it's for sale by the owner. Are you the agent or the owner?"

"This is the owner you are speaking with, Mr. Swazi. My name is Thomas Collins, but you can call me Tommy. We are not currently residing at Haven Court. We bought a townhouse in Downtown Boca. It's only been a month now since we moved and put the house up for sale. Our children are grown, and they are out on their own. It's just a bit humongous for us now."

"When can we meet to discuss business? My fiancée and I are very much interested."

"I must tell you, Peter, before we waste our time, that house is a bit pricey. It is a very large property. The house has all modern amenities and upgrades and sits on ten acres of land."

"Okay, Tommy, let's hear what you're asking when we meet. When do you think we could get together?"

Tommy suggested, "How about next Monday at two o'clock?"

"Next Monday would be just fine. I take it we will meet at the house address, 11 Haven Court. We would really like to see the inside."

"Yes, we will," Tommy responded.

The weekend was a rainy one; nevertheless, they had decided to attend the early morning mass at Saint Paul's Cathedral and to say a prayer for Aunt Stella. "The attendance was the best I have seen in a long time," Peter commented.

Father Hurling singled them out in his welcome observations and also announced their wedding for December 24. It was a touching sermon, a truly great exegesis of the parable of the five virgins. Father Hurling broke it down in layman's terms for all to understand. They truly enjoyed it.

Peter recognized a few of the parishioners and got a chance to greet them one-on-one. Some of them were still conveying their condolences with regard to his mother's passing and congratulated them on their engagement and imminent marriage in such a festive season. "It's the right time when everyone celebrates the birthday of the King."

They waited for Father Hurling to be free so they could verbally confirm their first counseling in September. He was quite elated to see them. And for sure, they were looking forward to their first counseling session.

It was not a long way from Saint Paul's to The Cliff. Peter thought they should have lunch there to show mutual respect and gratitude for their bombshell prize, which came at an excellent time. They had just opened for lunch when they arrived, with barely any parking spots available. Customers were already lined up, waiting to go in. The regular Sunday afternoon crowds seemed more than happy to dine; everyone was chatting and laughing, adding to the afternoon's enjoyment.

The rain came again just as they opened the doors, which hastened the seating. As fate would have it, they were privileged to sit at the same table on the lucky night of their win. It continued to rain, which brought on a chilly air mixed with the air-conditioning. The air was a lot crisper than usual. Peter offered Rose his jacket, the unexpected safeguard she thought she would not need. It was still summer, and the August heat was expected to rise again the very next day, according to the forecast.

"Well, we might as well place our order," Peter initiated.

"What do you suggest we eat?" Rose asked.

"Let's order something simple. They have a wide variety of dishes. They even have a signature lunch special."

"All right, how about house special soup and salad? You know that's always a great lunch. We have been heavy on our meals lately. Let's take a break with something light."

Peter raised his hand, signaling to the waiter they were ready to place the order. He picked up the menu and read to him what they desired. "Got you," the waiter said and then walked toward the computer where the orders were entered.

Out of the blue, there was a burst of lightning, and it was as if the heavens opened. There was a literal deluge of thunderstorms, with rain pouring down even harder than before. The electricity went out, resulting in an audible gasp from the patrons; miraculously, the generators ran, so there was also an audible sigh of relief.

"I am not comfortable at all with this, Peter. What if this happens the afternoon of our wedding reception?"

"Oh, Rose, you are such a worrywart. Why are you thinking that way? Everything will be okay. Notice there is a backup plan. See? We have electricity, and everything and everyone is functioning normally again."

They were served then, and for sure, the meal was a knockout. It was just totally great. There was no music, no band playing; everyone just enjoyed an atmosphere of privacy and minding their own business. "This is an undisturbed opportunity, Peter, for us to talk about how we should present our proposal on the house when we meet with Tommy tomorrow afternoon."

"How do you propose we go about acquiring the house, Rose? It's a huge property. Tommy might just price us out."

"Well, for sure, we are not making a cash purchase. It doesn't matter how great our financial position is. I suggest we get preapproved from a reputable lending institution for a short-term mortgage. We can establish credit that way. I am almost sure we will be approved based on our assets. I think we need to go now," Rose suggested. "It looks like the dinner guests are arriving, and we don't need to sit here any longer."

It was still raining when they got to the exit; this time, none of them had an umbrella. Peter had a really good chuckle as he recalled the night they met when Rose had to take shelter under his umbrella. "How about you wait here while I bring the car around? It doesn't make sense for both of us to get drenched with the rain."

In a minute, he was back. Between the raindrops, Rose rushed inside the car, and they had no choice but to slowly drive home because visibility was almost nonexistent. All the way, they held hands and prayed for their safety as the rain poured more; sudden thunderstorms began freaking them out. This was the type of weather that brought back so much memory in a scary way.

They did notice there were no streetlights on, and mostly, all the houses and some commercial buildings had no electricity either. Cautiously, they continued to Peter's house. He needed to collect a few items.

From a few feet away, they noticed that his sensors had no lights either. By the side of the garage, Peter had a cupboard that was built for emergencies where he secured things like candles, flashlights, matches, spare keys, water, and blankets. He pulled out a couple of large flashlights that were in perfect working condition. All was well inside except for a few drips here and there in areas damaged by the last storm that the carpenters had missed patching up.

Rose was quite sure when they got to her house that there would be no electricity either. But luckily, the power was still on. The entire neighborhood had electricity. "Thank God, Rose, we are home safely. A cup of coffee would be great in all this chaos."

Rose proceeded to check her cell phone and realized that she had missed a few calls from the hospital. It must have been during the time of the thunderstorm and the rain, but luckily, the doctor who attended to Aunt Stella left a message stating she was discharged under the care of a reputable nurse from the agency, who would be with her mostly during the day, and another would relieve her during the night. That was a bit of good news for Rose; she could relax, at least for now, and hope that all would go well even until after New Year.

She poured Peter's coffee, and then she poured a cup for herself. It was a very quiet evening for them to quietly talk about the wedding and all their plans, making sure they had invited most of their friends, crossing all the *t*'s and dotting all the *i*'s. "Let's also place a note on the calendar, Rose. We will need to apply for the marriage license at least by the first week in December. I believe it expires within thirty to ninety days after it's issued. Let's make a note of this and ask Father Hurling about the procedure when we meet for our first counseling session."

There was also another message for Rose that she would be having her first refresher driving lesson on Wednesday at ten o'clock. Peter decided he would accompany her. He was quite certain she would remember the rules of the road but just wanted to feel confident she could handle herself driving alone. The car was delivered and was parked in the garage; the driving instructor's message also stated he would be using her BMW to refresh her skills.

"What a difference a day makes!" Peter exclaimed, seeing the sunrise the next morning in comparison to last night's weather. "My, oh my, that was some rainfall we had last night. I can see how much the lawn perks up, and the flowers seem enthusiastic about every raindrop."

There were Florida Power and Light utility trucks at various locations, making the necessary repairs. The news reported most of the western side would receive power by the next day. That included where Peter's house was located.

The day slipped by uneventfully, and before they knew it, dinnertime had rolled around. Therefore, they decided to make their own. They had frozen dinners, but none of those would have been quite satisfying or were what they desired. They decided on chicken breast stuffed with steamed vegetables, which was the next best thing.

It was going to be a while before dinner would be ready as they would have to first defrost the chicken breast in the microwave. The air fryer would be the quickest way to have this ready in a tasty way. In the meantime, Peter prepared a side serving of roasted potatoes with mushrooms in the toaster oven. He also warmed up garlic bread, served with avocado paste, to be savored with dry red wine, which he placed in the refrigerator, giving it a soothing chilly taste.

"How are the chicken breasts coming along?" Peter inquired.

"They are almost done. Another few minutes, and they should be ready," Rose replied.

The table was already set. It looked quite romantic, with dim lighting along with lit candles. There was an aura of victory, celebration, and coziness. They positioned the meals in an inimitable setting. By then, their appetites grew more as they sat to enjoy a great entrée.

As the minutes went by, Peter said out loud, "We need to be on time for our meeting tomorrow with Tommy. The time we leave here will determine whether we will be on time."

"Depends on the time of day. I suggest we try to be ahead of the afternoon traffic."

"Therefore, young lady, my take is that we do an early night," Peter said while getting up from the table and kissing Rose on the forehead.

"You are so right." Rose quickly agreed as she cleared the dishes from the table and loaded them in the dishwasher. "We need to take a cold shower and sleep off all this wine we have consumed. My goodness, we had the entire bottle."

"Good night, my queen." Peter held Rose as they kissed good night. They reluctantly tore themselves apart and secretly wished they had not taken the chastity vow before marriage.

It was as if the night had only a few minutes. It seemed they fell asleep even before their heads got on the pillows. The next thing they knew, the sun was peeping through the shades.

The smell of coffee was always their alarm clock. Rose sat up in bed, anticipating her first sip. The table was already set with an arrangement of fresh fruits, scrambled eggs, turkey bacon, and toast.

Peter knocked. "Breakfast is served, Ms. Alexander."

Quickly, Rose freshened up and met him at the table. By the time they were through with breakfast, it was almost time to be on their way.

The traffic was moderately bearable; they got to 11 Haven Court on time. As a matter of fact, both couples arrived at the same time. The Collinses lived at their new home recently built in the suburbs of Boca Raton. According to Tommy, it was ordered a whole year before they were actually ready to start building. They waited awhile for the approval of the plan and the right time of year to commence building.

Tommy signaled Peter to park in the garage while he followed up the driveway. They took a few minutes to pray, asking God's direction on the conversation, believing all would go well.

"There is no furniture in the house. We left some chairs on the porch so the house would not seem unoccupied. We will do the walk-through first, and then we will sit down afterward if that's okay with everyone. The house has split levels," Tommy said. "From the outside, you couldn't tell. Let's begin in the living room on the first level."

It was a huge room, freshly painted with intricate crown molding. When they moved from room to room, they noticed they were all freshly painted, and every room boasted a signature theme. It was a gorgeous house in excellent condition. The walk-through took their breath away. In every room, the wood floors were made from cedar. Although there were no furnishings, the warm feeling of "home" was awesome and settling.

The house tour took quite a while, finally ending where they began, on the porch. "Sit down, guys. Let's talk business." Tommy reminded Peter of the conversation a couple of days ago. "I told you this house is a bit pricey. From the outside, you can see the landscaping, and the security of the land surrounding the house is like Fort Knox's. There are huge iron fences that appear like a fortress.

I asked you to park in the garage for you to have a feel of it. It's a three-car capacity with lots of storage shelves."

Just then, Tommy took Peter through a side door leading to the state-of-the-art kitchen that boasted cutting-edge appliances, floor-to-ceiling oak cabinets, and marble floors and countertops. This elegant kitchen opened into the garage. He pointed to a concealed pantry and all the conveniences for storage. "The gates to the property and the garage doors are controlled remotely, which automatically closes when you are securely inside the garage."

In the meantime, Betty, Tommy's wife, and Rose got into chatting as Betty described in glowing terms the benefits of having a home that size, especially if they were expecting to grow a new family. "Our girls are grown and are on their own, and for us to continue living in a house this size without a family is rather ridiculous. You both are young and have not even begun. This would suit you very well."

"Thank you, Mrs. Collins," Rose replied. "I wholeheartedly agree."

Tommy and Peter joined the ladies on the porch again as they continued the business at hand. "The entire house, from the front entrance all the way in, is armed with sensors and cameras," Tommy reiterated. "We use the best security system in Boca, with the central station working in tandem with the Boca Police Station. I will let you have all their information, and the next time you are downtown, let me know in advance so I can introduce you. Of course, you will need a new password and code." Tommy chuckled. "Well, what do you think, Rose, Peter? Are you satisfied with what you've seen so far?"

"Of course," they both replied.

"Let us hear your asking price, and then we will know if we really love the house," Rose said with a wink.

"We are asking $3.5 million with $0.5 million as a down payment. You don't have to worry about getting a lending institution to borrow from to pay the mortgage. We will hold it. And by the way, we have further decided to give both of you $0.5 million as your wedding gift."

Rose grabbed Peter's hand in disbelief, trying to suppress her excitement and not wanting to appear overenthusiastic. They were filled with exhilaration and delight; it was hard for them to express the gratefulness of the unexpected gift.

Tommy and Betty excused themselves to give Peter and Rose a chance to deliberate. A half-hour passed before they returned with the question.

Chapter 11

"What have you two decided?" Tommy inquired.

Peter looked with a visibly questioning expression. "When can we close this deal?" he asked. "The price is fine with us." They had deliberated on the price for a while and had decided that since they were getting a cash wedding gift from the Collinses, they would accept the offer.

Without verbalizing it, Peter and Rose were prepared to go as high as four million but kept silent at the offer price. "We don't know how to thank you for your generosity and your benevolence," Peter said with such gratitude. "The wedding gift is beyond belief. We will use the funds to furnish the house. We have asked God to perpetually bless you and your endeavors."

"How about we close next Monday, a week from today? I will message my attorney, Mr. Daniel Huss, and have him set up an appointment for twelve o'clock if that time is convenient. You can also have your attorney present to make sure all goes well, or we can use one attorney. This way, we all win."

"Oh wow!" Peter exclaimed. "I see we have the same attorney, Tommy, Daniel Huss. He was my mother's attorney when she purchased our house. He's a very conscious attorney who is fair, knowledgeable in real estate transactions, and honest. He is highly respected everywhere. I will contact him myself, for old time's sake. I know he will oblige us. It's been many years since we have spoken, but one thing I know, he has a great memory. He will also instruct me about what documents I will need to bring to the closing."

Tommy jokingly said, "At least the attorney's fees will not be for two people. That's a great advantage."

Driving home, for the most part of the way, none of them spoke. They just held hands and could not contain the tears. Peter began thanking God for His unsearchable gift of love and for His unadulterated blessings, which they could not understand. The drive seemed longer than the way they came when they started out for 11 Haven Court, all because they were not in any hurry. They just enjoyed the moment in gratefulness and love.

They needed a quiet night to party, waiting for reality to set in, making sure tomorrow, when they awoke, it was not a dream. "Let's call one of the nearby restaurants that do deliveries to bring us something. The feeling of celebration quietly is tempting and welcoming. After all, we are deserving of it."

Peter turned into the driveway and shut the engine off, and they just sat there. "Rose, I am sure we thought the house was going to be far more than the offer they gave us, at least $4 million, right? It's not that we could not afford to buy that house for cash, but let's not be too transparent with our finances."

"Do you think when we get into that meeting on Monday, we could arrange for four equal payments on the balance? Would that bring transparency to our assets, Peter? I know we would like to make a one-time payment, but that's what we are trying to avoid: the question, right? I just cannot bear the thought of being in debt. If we pay the whole amount, there will be questions. And even though we have nothing to hide, we do not need the questions or raised eyebrows," Rose answered.

"Yes, of course, we can do that."

"I think we both could settle that amount that way, Peter. Do you think it will pose a question on the gift they gave us?" Rose questioned.

"Let's sleep on all this. In the morning, we will decide."

Everything was quickly falling into place; they could hardly keep up with the pace of how everything was going. "This is a good sign for us, Rose, that God is leading every step of the way. Here we are. In a few days, we will be selecting furniture for our new home. After Monday's closing and we are given the keys, I would suggest, Rose, we hire an interior decorator to come in, walk them through the house, listen carefully to their suggestions, and in the meantime, give them ours. I have made a mental note of the changes I would like to make and our color scheme for each room. We will go over these before I introduce them to the decorators. But we need to start as soon as possible.

"There is so much for us to do before the wedding. That's why I suggest we definitely need additional help. There is no way we can decorate the house and prepare for our wedding simultaneously. The good thing is we do not have to decorate The Cliff or the church. They need no additional decoration, and that is a big plus. We only need to concentrate on the house."

It was not long after they placed the dinner order that the doorbell rang. Peter always said, "I'll get it." Rose got the dining table prepared for dining.

It would seem as though there was something to celebrate every day these days. "If we do not let up on the wine consumption, pretty soon, we will have to commit ourselves to rehab," Peter said with a loud laugh. "Or we might just get carried away emotionally." This sobered up both Rose and Peter, so they decided that, from now on, they would stick to sparkling cider unless they had company or dined out.

It was already two hours into the next day. After much thought and prayer, they decided secretly on the best way to handle the questions (if asked) of Mr. and Mrs. Thomas Collins' pricey gift to them and their comfortable financial position. For the little they knew of Tommy and Betty Collins, they seemed to be of much worth and could not care less one way or another who would pose that question. A gift of half a million seemed much, but that was the kind of people they were, which is obvious among their friends and close acquaintances.

Yes, they were aware they had not known them for a long time, and they were also cognizant of the fact that they knew Peter and Rose could use the money for their wedding anyway. They both had the spirit of benevolence and knew that it could make the difference between a regular, run-of-the-mill wedding and an exquisite one, especially at this time when they knew, as experienced parents with married children, that this was an enormous and expensive undertaking. "Let's not squander any more time on this subject, Rose. There are weightier matters for us to deal with. Have you ever seen the David's Bridal advertisement on television, Rose? They are having wedding specials, such as dresses, tuxedos, and other wedding paraphernalia at their Downtown Boca location."

"No, I haven't," she replied.

"Let's see if, by any chance, they may have the selections we need for our wedding. Time is of the essence, and we have only a few months to go," was Peter's suggestion.

"I think we should give Abigail a call and have her meet us there. They might have just what she is looking for."

"Whatever we accomplish in any given day is worth the effort." Sure enough, Rose, Peter, and Abigail were quite satisfied in obtaining their wedding outfit without a doubt.

They were reluctant to order dinner before they took a nap. If they did, for sure, they would sleep through the ringing and knocking of the doorbell when the delivery came. "Are you up, honey?" Rose yelled from across the hall. "I am ordering dinner. What would you like to eat tonight? I am getting ready to place the order."

Peter came out in his robe, rubbing his eyes and yawning loudly. "Look at you, Rose!" he exclaimed with a loud laugh.

"I am all nice and casual, and you are in your robe, yawning away, looking all tussled and rumpled just like a precocious little boy. It's not that kind of party, Peter. It's dinnertime." Rose made light of the moment.

"Okay, the future Mrs. Swazi, I will be right back to place my order." He chuckled and turned back toward his room. Peter went in for a minute and then came out looking really smart. He reminded Rose of when they first met and would get all dolled up for each other.

What they wanted for dinner was not available as it was past eight o'clock, and the kitchen was closed. The waiter took the order after he informed them of the fastest and easiest entrée consisting of hamburgers with homemade french fries and a side of lettuce and tomato with mustard on the side so they could make their own sandwiches. They were too hungry not to place the order.

"We are not having wine tonight," Peter warned. "Remember my advice a few days ago. Let's avoid so much wine." He feared them getting addicted without even thinking. "Tomorrow will be your first refresher driving class."

Rose nervously nodded and went to the refrigerator for a drink. "Are you coming with me, Peter?" Rose asked sharply.

"Yes, I am," he responded. "And you are advised to be there on time. These instructors have quite a bit of a lineup. Make sure you have your license and any other type of identification that might be required."

Dinner was delivered; it was so well organized, with two slices of complimentary carrot cake on the side for dessert—a treat from the chef. He added a note under the napkins, which read, "If you enjoyed the cake, please tell others. If not, please tell us."

"That's a nice gesture, Peter," Rose said as she finished setting up the table. Peter walked toward her and stretched his arm out to lend a helping hand.

"I got this," Rose said with a girlish gesture. "It's not much to get done." They both settled down and enjoyed a simple dinner. They commented on how tasty it was.

It seemed like a long night for Rose's driving course the next day. "Oh, Peter, I barely slept last night. I feel panicky. You need to pray that I do well."

Peter held his fiancée and prayed that the fear would dissipate by the time they got started.

At the end of the lesson, she asked, "Well, how did I do?"

"You did excellent, Rose. After that prayer, I am not surprised you did so well. I knew you would not be nervous, to say the least. You handled yourself like a pro. I would say, just one more lesson, and you will be fine."

The next day, the instructor was available for one last lesson, which went well. He told the owner, Mr. Ben Scott, of Rose's progress, of which he was delighted. Ben sent Rose a congratulatory message, telling her how proud he was to hear of her advancement. "You have done well," he said. "I told you you could do it. You have conquered the fear, and now you are ready to have your independence. God has not given you the spirit of fear, Rose, but of power and of love and of a sound mind. Please do not forget that."

As was planned, the next day, they met with Mr. and Mrs. Collins and Atty. Daniel Huss at the property and not at the attorney's office for the closing. In advance, Peter had asked that if it would not pose a problem, he would prefer to have the closing at 11 Haven Court. "We would make use of the opportunity to give Mr. Huss an idea of the house as he is an old friend of the family, and I am familiar with his criticisms in whichever way, after working along with my mother and me in the past."

"Of course, it was not a problem. He is also a friend and family attorney for the Collinses for many years."

Mr. Huss discussed his findings; everything was transparent, exceptionally amicable, and businesslike to the minutest detail. Peter asked, as was discussed, if, in the agreement, they could make four equal payments, once per year for four years, to complete the debt earlier than the expected arrangements of ten years they had thought of.

"Of course," the attorney replied. "If that's what you both are asking, I am in total agreement. Anything you desire, we are here to work along with you."

He turned to Mr. and Mrs. Collins to ask their thoughts on the payment arrangement as they were the ones holding the mortgage, and they were definitely delighted to accommodate them. They unabashedly expressed their thoughts that Peter and Rose were the perfect couple for the home they loved so much.

Everything went well. The agreement was written and signed by the seller and the buyer, and closure was brought to the property at 11 Haven Court. It was a pleasure for Tommy and Betty to hand over the keys to Peter and Rose, congratulating them on their acquisition.

Happily, Peter and Rose drove away feeling quite accomplished but then had a discussion about what they would do with the houses they now owned. The thought of selling came to mind. Peter, on second thought, decided against selling because real estate is what everyone desires to keep as an appreciating investment. "We could speak to Mr. Huss after the honeymoon and present him with a proposal for management of our real estate properties and focus on renting to executives from state government offices, city government offices, or municipal services. Or we can just make them into bed-and-breakfast conveniences or rent them as just furnished homes."

A furnished house is convenient for anyone renting and who does not have the money or desire to go furniture shopping. Rose's house was just about a year old, tastefully furnished, and well-kept enough for anyone to live comfortably and in a calm, pleasant atmosphere.

"I am sure going to miss that roof," Rose mentioned to Peter. "They built it experimenting on how the sound of the raindrops would ricochet like musical entertainment."

"I understand, Rose, but let's take care of all that as soon as we come through all these critical and pressing engagements."

Peter pulled over and suggested that Rose drive to Father Hurling's as an encouragement for her to practice as much driving as possible and get used to the roads. It was their first counseling session, which went well. Rose also drove to the remaining sessions and did great.

With the wedding within weeks away, Rose's phone reminder prompted her that they needed to collect the marriage license. The next day, they were first in line at the city hall. It took them about an hour to acquire it, but thank God they did.

On their way home, they decided to stop at Saint Paul's Cathedral and deliver the license to Father Hurling. They knew they were a bit early in delivering it, but it was more convenient to leave it then than later. They were intensely executing their time well to avoid the holiday rush they could see brewing.

Thanksgiving was in a few days, and of course, that was when the official holiday season began. Peter and Rose thought of how they would spend Thanksgiving—quietly at either of their homes or utilizing that time to acquire work at their new home or do Christmas shopping. Ben and Sheila Scott had sent them an invitation to have dinner at their house, where they could meet their children with their families instead of being alone.

On their way home, they noticed a sign that read, "Interior decorators, inquire within."

"Let's stop for a minute, Peter, and see what they are offering. We might just engage them to deal with the entire decor for our new house, along with the holidays."

The company had a great entranceway, going down the corridor, leading to the actual inside of the office. They were enjoying the homeliness and the way they designed and arranged the furniture, which gave the look of a beautifully decorated home. They were sold already just from the way the sample decor was presented.

From the hanging certificates, they could see it was family-owned. The owners were retired realtors, husband and wife, along with their children, who became realtors and also ran the business. After a short consultation, Peter and Rose made arrangements with Mrs. Majors to meet them the next day at their house for a walk-through and an estimate.

Rose told Peter how proud he made her feel with his thoughtfulness and extraordinary pizzazz to suggest an interior decorator to take the load off. "It would have been too much for me to be responsible for getting the entire house together in such a short time. I know, Peter, you would have interesting contributions on the furniture and color scheme, but the bulk would be on me, deciding what goes where in the various rooms."

The house was in such great condition, from the porch to the inside, that there was nothing to do but paint, change the room color, and move in. Somehow, the enormity of it was overwhelming and panicky. By then, it was midafternoon when they left the decorator's store, and Peter suggested that Rose continue to drive and get acquainted with the car on the road. He felt a bit sleepy, and she could visibly see him dozing a few times.

She was approaching a bend in the road and quickly read a sign saying, "Falling rocks." Just then, out of nowhere, a boulder became loose from the side of a hill and began rolling toward them. Rose's first instinct was to immediately stop but could not as there were other cars close behind them. She became frantic and began screaming for Peter.

By then, Rose was really hysterical, and in a split second, the car was out of control. She managed to grab the steering wheel again and maneuvered away from a head-on collision with oncoming vehicles.

Before she knew it, the BMW was hanging over a ravine where the river ran beneath. The car had flipped, and they were both hanging upside down with the entire front bumper torn completely off.

Rose started becoming really groggy as she fought to stay awake, even though the odor of gasoline was overpowering. She struggled hard to remain conscious, telling herself that she might have a concussion and that sleeping would amplify the adverse effect. She could hear Peter yelling for help as if he was far away in the distance.

Many motorists stopped to assist but were afraid to even make an effort to get near the doors due to the position the car was in. Rose observed that the slightest touch would cause chaos, devastation, and maybe death. Even a very strong gust of wind could tip the car over and into the river. In a few minutes, the rescue trucks were there, along with firefighters and the Florida police. The traffic jam was horrendous as the traffic officer tried to keep vehicles moving and the roadway clear.

It was the job of the firefighters to have the crane lowered, cradling the car to pull it to safety. Everyone's prayer was for both passengers to be all right. The car was lifted to safety as other motorists gawked to see what had caused the devastation. However, the boulder was still in the middle of the road, which made it difficult for the traffic to go around it.

Peter was first pulled out and carried to the ambulance. He was bleeding from his nose with bruises and contusions possibly obtained from the deployment of the airbags. Then, all efforts were made to reach in to get a hold of Rose. The car had to be cut apart, but thank God the firefighters, working alongside the rescue team, got it done and extricated Rose from the wreckage. She was disoriented and undoubtedly terrified, holding her head and muttering what could be heard as a prayer. The ambulance sped off for the hospital while the onlookers talked among themselves and suggested they say a prayer that they would be fine.

Father Hurling received quite a few calls from the parishioners who had recognized Rose and Peter, which impelled him to be at the hospital as soon as possible. They were rushed through the emergency entrance and immediately taken into the rooms to be triaged. The doctors did their evaluation, examining various X-rays and scans. They were amazed, after hearing the magnitude of the crash, that they both did not have more severe injuries.

Rose obtained multiple cuts and bruises to her hands and neck and was suffering from gasoline inhalation. The boulder had actually punctured the gas tank. Peter had a concussion but was expected to recover in a few days. Both Rose and Peter were admitted for observation and treatment.

Father Hurling was allowed inside the rooms, where he quickly prayed for their fast and safe recovery. Although their conditions were not life-threatening, they were not out of the woods completely. The head physician told Father Hurling they would be kept for a few days under keen observation in case there were aftereffects.

Chapter 12

It took the doctors four days to discharge Peter and Rose from the Boca Medical Center. They wanted to make sure all their tests were negative and that they weren't in any immediate physical danger. The couple took an Uber from the hospital to home.

The driver had to travel in the same direction, passing the location where they had the accident. It was unbelievable that the car was still there. They understood it was advised that the car should remain there for a few days while the authorities and insurance company did a thorough investigation. Looking at the wreckage brought a fresh reminder of what happened four days ago. They both were saddened but were also encouraged and thankful that they were able to physically walk away with just minor injuries.

Getting out of the Uber and walking into the house was like a breath of fresh air. "Thank God!" Peter exclaimed. "Who would have known we would miraculously make it back home after such an exciting closing on the home we bought and love so much? We almost missed out on living in it. This scripture came to mind: 'Behold, Satan hath desired to have you, that he may sift you as wheat.'[6] That's

---

6   "And the Lord said, Simon, Simon, behold, Satan hath desired *to have* you, that he may sift *you* as wheat" (Luke 22:31, KJV).

what the enemy desires to do with us, Rose. Hadn't God stepped in and blocked it, the situation would have been disastrous."

"'Thanks be to God, who gives us the victory, through our Lord Jesus Christ.'"

Taking a long hot shower was a welcome undertaking. Peter suggested that they each indulge in a long hot bath. Rose agreed, and they both walked away to their separate bathrooms. "Make sure that you add some Epsom salt to the bathwater!" Rose yelled. "You can find it in the cabinet directly under the sink."

They were so excited to be able to talk about the accident, which was no fault of any of them. Rose was still a little unhinged, and every now and again, she would whimper when she remembered the whole ordeal. Peter had to continuously restore confidence and remind her of how much he loved her and that she would be fine. She, in turn, thanked him for his love and understanding through the entire conundrum.

Father Hurling promised to visit with them later on the same day they returned home from the hospital. About two hours after they emerged from their well-appreciated baths, they were surprised by the ringing of the doorbell. It was Father Hurling; seeing him made such a difference. He proved to be a really caring and passionate person, filled with empathy and love.

To their surprise, Father Hurling brought them dinner from one of their favorite restaurants, along with other delicious and delectable delicacies. "This is much appreciated, Father Hurling. We really do not take this frivolously. It is really giving of yourself. You have proved to us that you really embody spiritual fatherhood. You are a great guy," Peter told him with a hearty handshake. "We hope and pray we will also be there for you in times of need."

Father Hurling prayed with them and made himself accessible. "If ever you needed anything, please feel free to ask."

Peter's phone rang; it was Ben Scott. "Hey, Peter, how are you two coming along? Are you still in the hospital, or are you at home? I heard of the accident."

"We are home," Peter replied.

Ben continued, "Peter, one of my employees happened to be in the area and recognized the white BMW only by the license plate. Thank God you both are alive and doing well. You are spared because of him. He has protected you both from what could have been a disaster. Once in a blue moon, those rocks become loose, and history tells us it's never always a good outcome. Consider yourselves blessed. Don't worry; I have gone ahead and notified the insurance company. They are asking for the police report, which I have already requested. One of my guys will collect it tomorrow."

"Thank you so much, Ben. You took a load off. I will pass on all this information to Rose. I am sure that will help her convalesce faster."

"And by the way, Peter, don't worry. When you both have settled your nerves, I will still be able to do something for you. I know it will be a challenge for Rose, but she will eventually get over it. This is all a part of life."

They finally settled down to dinner and had already decided to unwind at home with a good night's sleep—not watching TV, not playing any games, not even making phone calls, of which they had a backlog. Their mailboxes were full, but getting better was most important at this time. It was one of the best nights to give thanks, commune with God, and not be ungrateful for His protection and care.

"I know we are still sore and panicky, having a few visible bandages here and there. But if tomorrow we're up to it, Rose, we could make a trip down to our new house just to look around. Maybe being there will definitely help lift our spirits."

Rose just nodded and then leaned against Peter's chest to be appeased. They went to bed early, as was decided.

Before they knew it, it was daybreak; they passed the night well and even slept in quite late. There were a few complaints of soreness here and there, but that was taken care of with pain meds. Peter made a great breakfast. Rose exclaimed it was so good; it would definitely stick to the ribs, and it was all gone before they knew it.

"Peter, it feels as though we have not eaten in quite a few days." They were making fun of how hungry they were. "I am not ready to go anywhere," Rose said honestly. "I am suggesting we take the weekend off just to recuperate."

Peter readily agreed. In any event, they both decided to go for regular morning and afternoon walks.

Tension could still be felt between them; every so often, they envisioned the boulder rolling down from the side of the hill. Rose was still frightened and kept having nightmares of the accident. She screamed at times as though she was reliving the whole accident. Father Hurling visited regularly, counseling and praying with them for a quick recovery.

The weekend did them much good; they did timely and quiet walks, meditated, and prayed, which helped divert their minds from the accident and gave them time to discuss the wedding and the home decorations. They had to reschedule a new date for the decorator.

As often as possible, the doctor made his calls from the hospital, making sure they were on their way to complete healing and recovery. Healing was now in the forefront; Peter and Rose were returning to normalcy. In the interim, they managed to fully furnish the house to a comfortable start. The decorators did a great job, from drapes, curtains, and rugs to the minutest details to Peter and Rose's satisfaction. The job was superbly done to their taste.

Tommy had introduced Peter to the monitoring company, which came and reset the codes and alarms. The landscaper, with good recommendation, continued to do his job on the property as was agreed; they also met and liked him very much. Peter and Rose were also introduced to their immediate neighbors, who welcomed them to the neighborhood with baked apple pies and chocolate chip cookies.

The travel agency was among the many missed calls during the time they were incapacitated. They gave the name of Ben Scott to the agency. In case there were any emergencies, and they could not be reached, he would be the fittest person to act on their behalf. As fate would have it, he was contacted and was able to confirm the itinerary after going over everything.

"It's a good thing we had made our deposits." Peter smiled gleefully. "It's a sure decision. Dubai is where we want to go."

The travel agency wanted them to know that the documents were ready to be picked up. It was necessary for them to make sure everything was done according to their last discussion and that there would be no misunderstanding with the airlines they selected, the preferred seating, first class as was requested, and the five-star hotel with the types of suggested activities and excursions.

Ben did an excellent job overall. He was very familiar with the Dubai trips; he had been there so many times and knew that the Christmas holidays were the best time to visit. He was wholeheartedly happy that they had decided on one of the best places for their honeymoon, as was suggested.

Everything seemed okay as they had anticipated. There were a number of dos and don'ts. They had a bit of shopping to do according to the list that was included with their itinerary. This was their first trip together, so they needed quite a lot of stuff.

Between the both of them, they had some old suitcases that needed to be replaced. Of course, shopping took them quite a while, getting what was necessary, but they loved it anyway. The excitement of getting away for two whole weeks to an unknown country had them animated.

They googled and researched a lot about Dubai, especially its culture, how the natives operated, their way of life, the restaurants, and even the dunes. They heard so much about the world's biggest shopping mall and the world's biggest flower garden, but more so, they were looking forward to visiting the Burj Khalifa and admiring the different types of lights at night. They could not wait to visit there in person.

Everything was set for the honeymoon; the suitcases were packed and set aside according to the guidelines as requested by the travel agency. Of course, adequate room remained for any last-minute addition to their vacation wardrobe. Their flight would leave at seven o'clock on Christmas night; they anxiously looked forward to boarding one of the largest airlines, Emirates, and they were told they would be flying for at least sixteen hours.

"We are more excited about the honeymoon trip than the wedding," Peter said with a wide grin, and every so often, they would look at each other with excitement when they remembered the trip. "All right, Rose, let's focus now on the wedding day. It's only a few days away, and there are some loose ends."

The doctor called earlier, reminding them of their appointment that same day for their checkup just to make sure they would be okay for their wedding and honeymoon trip and that they were not in any impending danger. They arrived at the hospital ten minutes ahead of schedule, and as luck would have it, they were seen right away. After careful examination, it was confirmed that both of them had made good progress toward healing and recovery and were given clearances for their everyday activities.

On their way home from the hospital, Rose thought it would be a good idea to give Aunt Stella a call. The home help answered the phone and gave a good report on how she was coming along. "Where is she?" Rose inquired.

"She is taking her afternoon nap and will be up in an hour. I will let her know you called. If it's not a problem, could you give her a call after dinner? About five o'clock?"

"Of course," Rose replied and ended the call.

"Aren't you hungry?" Peter asked.

Rose was scratching at her eyes as if to say she would prefer to take a nap instead of eating.

He reached across and held her hand. "Come on, let's stop at the next diner. We might as well start our eating-out habit early. After all, the wedding is only days away. Then, for the next two weeks after December 24, it will be every day, three meals a day if we desire."

Rose agreed and said with a broad smile, "I could get used to that. I am also looking forward to the spa. I really need a good body massage, and for you, Peter, you need to get into the gym for a good workout. Don't you think that would do us good?"

"After such a frightening accident, we need to be pampered somehow. I think you were the hardest hit, Rose," Peter said. "My God! We are blessed to be alive. I don't think two weeks will be enough. Let's see when we arrive if the country is anything like we've read about and holds to the recommendations of Ben. Then we will request an extra week as long as it's convenient and available all the way around the board."

For whatever reason, their spirits were lifted. They felt as if Jesus loved them more than anyone else, looking back over all that they had been through and how he stood by them. His promises are sure and unwavering. He said:

Be strong and of good courage,
Fear not, nor be afraid of them:
for the Lord thy God. He it is that doth go with thee;
He will not fail thee, nor forsake thee.

Deuteronomy 31:6 (KJV)

As the wedding day drew near, the butterflies started fluttering in their stomachs, and the excitement grew more and more. Every day, they were making sure that everything was in place. Peter would call The Cliff, inquiring if there was anything they needed in addition to what they had provided before the wedding day, December 24. The managing team's representative, Suzan, read all that they had provided to Rose, inclusive of the cake and favors. She was contented with their gift, which was extremely admirable.

"Thank you, Suzan. We will see you in a few days. If there are any new adjustments, please feel free to contact us."

It was commendable that during the time of courtship, the closing of both inheritances, the purchase of their new home, and the wedding plans, from the tiniest iota to the greatest decision, Peter and Rose had never had a financial disagreement. Their prayer was, "Lord, unite us to see each of us as one. May we live together in perfect harmony."

This should be the prayer of every new couple commencing a new life. There should be a solid foundation of a frequent prayer life, putting God first. There should always be a level of transparency. The hide-and-seek deception should not be a part of the union. There should be frequent and honest communication about the future; there should also be deep attraction and love between the couple and hope for a lasting relationship since one of the reasons many marriages fall apart is that they start off with the wrong agenda. Peter and Rose were levelheaded Christians, and with the direction of the triune God, their lives would be an example.

Father Hurling's secretary called to say he was asking them to meet with him as soon as possible. They were aware they had done all the required time of counseling, but he needed to talk with them one final time to make sure they had covered all the bases and that there would be no missteps.

The nature of the meeting went just as they thought. Father Hurling took them inside the sanctuary to familiarize them with where they would enter and exit. He also asked that they do a quick rehearsal two days before the wedding. "We all need to be on the same page," he said with a chuckle.

It was still early in the afternoon. Rose had enough time to send a reminder to the bridal party of the time they needed to be at the church for rehearsal the next day. Father Hurling needed them to be on time as he had another engagement immediately after. She also sent a reminder to the florist of the time they needed to have the arrangements delivered. She made sure to give them the new home address.

Rose suggested they should have the decorators come back and do light Christmas decorations inside and also install a very large Christmas tree in the middle of the lawn. They were the new kids on the block and would like to share the same sentiment of the season as others. Most of their personal items were already at 11 Haven Court. Just a few sentimental pieces were left, which they planned to collect after the wedding and honeymoon.

Unexpectedly, Peter began pouring his heart out to Rose; he began by saying, "Rose, please allow me." He held her hand. "I really wished our parents were here to share with us what will be the happiest moments of our lives, Rose. Life plays us differently from what we had anticipated. The people who brought us into the world for a God-given purpose were taken from us under tragic circumstances. Now, here we are, two hearts that beat as one."

"I have always envisioned as you have, Rose, seeing myself walking down the aisle of Saint Paul's Cathedral one day. So I am envisioning what would have been such joy in having our parents here in attendance on our wedding day, even to light a unity candle and throw rice at us as in days gone by. I love you, Rose. I did not have to grow to love you. From that stormy afternoon when you were rescued under my umbrella from a brutal storm, you also came into my heart, my life, the one I found to be irresistible. We have encountered so much entanglement that could have tarnished our love. It appeared sometimes I had lost you, but no, we are still here."

"I have never verbalized this, Rose, but I feel I have to do this before I answer Father Hurling when I am asked if I would take this woman to love and to hold. When I say I do, it must be said with a light heart. Therefore, I am emptying myself so I can be relieved of all the shenanigans and be completely transparent to move forward. Are you following me, Rose?"

"Yes, Peter, I am following you," she replied with tears in her eyes.

Peter continued, "When Aunt Stella began acting weird, she thought I only wanted you because of your father's inheritance. I was driven to dejection. I came to the brink of calling it quits. I began telling myself to forget about this whole love thing. It clearly wasn't working in my favor."

"Here I am with a beautiful woman whom I love so much, but I am despised by her only living relative, her aunt. I was frustrated. I became delusional. But in the middle of my confusion, I heard in my spirit a voice speaking to me: 'For I know the plans I have for you, declares the Lord, plans to prosper you and not to harm you, plans to give you hope and a future.'[7] That's all I needed to hear. I know that was the voice of God, Rose, and in the middle of absolute disgruntlement, I was now on the runway, ready to take off to a future of hope filled with plans and prosperity. That's what I meant to say a few days ago. I can see things falling into place."

"I am glad I had not fallen in love with you for your inheritance. I didn't know I had mine without either of us knowing about it. That's

---

7   "'For I know the plans I have for you,' declares the LORD, 'plans to prosper you and not to harm you, plans to give you hope and a future'" (Jeremiah 29:11, NIV).

enough to suffice both of us for many years to come, and on top of that, God has blessed us. I am finished, Rose."

With that said, Peter held Rose close to him and allowed her to know this was how he felt about her.

"You have spoken well, Peter. I know all that you have said isn't mere hyperbole. I know for sure you are earnest, and this gives me fresh eyes to see the journey ahead of us. I am free from the weight I have been carrying for all these months. It had crossed my mind so many times to ask if you were happy and comfortable with everything, but I was apprehensive to say something. Really, everything has fallen into place.

"Again, I feel like the weight of a freight train has been lifted off my shoulders. That was a rather intense and, at the same time, comforting discourse, Peter. I love you so much for your honesty. Thank you for spilling your guts. I perceive, after all that you have said, that you must have gained the necessary fortitude concerning the plans God has for us. Ready, steady, let's go."

Chapter 13

December 24—yes, the day before Christmas—was here, the day of their nuptials. When Rose first entered Saint Paul's Cathedral on a sightseeing tour, she concluded that one day, she would literally walk down the aisle. Who would have thought the day would come in reality?

The air was filled with celebratory carols and decorations on almost every house as far as one could see. They all had front door Christmas murals. All the lampposts had red ornaments, cascading Christmas garlands, and "Deck the Halls" wreaths, to name a few. The scenery was festively awesome. Every inch of Boca Raton was making a Christmas proclamation. The stores were beautifully decorated with variations of Christmas lights that all twinkled in rhythmic synchronization.

The air was a wafting conglomerate of aromatic pies, pastries, Italian pizza, popcorn, and cotton candy. Restaurants were busy preparing for various celebrations. Shoppers were busy in the streets, popping in and out of stores, getting their last-minute gifts and shopping done.

Peter and Rose nonchalantly decided just to drive into town with one thing in mind: window-shop. It was what the old folks called "grand market shopping" or "the night-before-Christmas pickings."

It was a challenge not to nip into the stores. The temptation was very strong. But they had bought everything they needed, and the special gifts were bought with instructions to the store workers to deliver on Christmas Day.

So they held hands and walked until they found themselves standing in front of Jared Jewelers when Peter suddenly gasped, "Rose, the ring! We have not gotten the rings! Oh my goodness!"

"It would be funny if it wasn't so serious," Peter said when Rose began roaring with laughter. She had not remembered either. "It's not even funny, Rose. Let's go inside. We must buy something right now, or we would be up a creek without a paddle. Good grief, what if we hadn't decided to go for a drive, Rose?"

This was the argument they had while pushing the door as they entered the store. The store manager politely asked if he could help with anything. "Sure, we are hoping you would." Peter reluctantly spoke to him. "I feel awful for what I am about to tell you, but we are getting married tomorrow afternoon, and because of so many reasons, which we do not have enough time to share with you, the rings were the last thing on our minds. Had we not found ourselves standing in front of your store, we would not have realized we have no rings for the ceremony."

It was a good thing Rose was wearing her engagement ring, which made it easy to find a match. The manager found it very fascinating but tried his best to conceal his amazement. "Okay, come over here. I might just have the right rings for both of you." He pulled out two trays and placed them on the counter in front of them. Those were not anything they were looking for.

"Are there any others?" Rose asked.

"Yes," he replied. "But the others are a bit pricey."

They both looked at each other when the manager walked over to another showcase as if to say, *I am sure these will be out of your budget.* This time, he had to use a key to open that showcase. "These I can only display one at a time."

"We are fine with that. What's your name, may I ask?" Rose inquired.

"My name is Matthew, but everyone calls me Matt for short," he said with a sharp smile as if to say, *Don't waste my time.*

"May I have a look at your engagement ring, please, if you don't mind?" Matt asked.

"Sure," Rose responded as she raised her left hand, positioning it up to his eyes.

While doing that, both Rose and Peter pointed to the rings they liked as Matt hesitantly picked them up and reluctantly presented them to them one by one. There were no price tags attached; it seemed the price was written at the bottom of the boxes. The rings they selected caused Matt to raise an eyebrow. "Wow!" he exclaimed. "You both have chosen two of the most expensive rings in the showcase. Are you sure you really want to buy these?"

In the meantime, Peter and Rose tried the rings for size, and as luck would have it, they were the perfect fit. "Can you have them steamed for us, please?"

Matt took both rings and walked to the back. They did not bother to ask what the cost was as they were fully aware this was the final chance to secure their rings for tomorrow's nuptial, and Matt did not volunteer any information.

In a few minutes, a beautiful white-haired woman appeared with a receipt book. She opened a small wooden gate and invited them in. They were shown to an old, antique table with really smart-looking chairs kind of matching. "Sit down," she invited them. "My name is Alice. I am the store owner."

"Nice meeting you," they both responded. "I am Peter, and this is my fiancée, Rose. Matt may have told you how absentminded we have been. We both overlooked the rings. Thank God we decided to drive into town tonight just to walk around and window-shop. Also, we needed a break from all we had been doing. And as they say, the rest is history."

Alice sat back in the old mahogany chair, switching the pen from one finger to the next, and then spoke. "These rings are very expensive, you know. I just think I should let you know the price before we go any further."

Peter interrupted, "With all due respect, Alice, will you please let us have the prices so we can be on our way? We don't want to be out too late as we are getting married tomorrow, and there are bits and pieces we need to get together tonight. Thank you."

Alice wrote the prices on the receipt book and gave it to Peter with a doubtful look; Peter thanked her and asked, "Are they ready?"

She hurriedly walked to the back, calling for Matthew. "Hurry with the rings, dear."

Peter reached into his coat pocket and then pulled out his debit card, and paid for them both. It would appear as though Alice was at a loss for words. The diamonds were brilliantly shining when Alice placed them in some unusually designed ring boxes, wrapped them delicately, and then shoved them down to the bottom of one medium shopping bag with the name Jared Jewelers written on the outside. She thanked them profusely, and for an added thank-you wedding gift, she gave Rose a mother-of-pearl necklace with matching earrings; and to Peter, she gave fragrance by Malone. They were escorted to the door and thanked again with hearty congratulations on the beginning of their new journey together.

Peter and Rose walked briskly to the red Bentley, which was parked within blocks of the jewelry store, and decided they would not stop for any window shopping even if they had four flat tires. "I am feeling a bit hungry, Rose. Can you call for a light dinner, please, that by the time we get home, it will almost be there?"

"Of course, Peter, what do you feel like having?"

"See if they have shrimp lo mein with vegetables."

"Good choice," Rose agreed. "But you know, that's not a light dinner." She chuckled. "That's mouth-watering just thinking about it."

They had not remembered that all their toiletries were taken to their new house. It was decided they would spend the night before their wedding in their separate homes, but it just didn't work that way.

Everything was on automatic at 11 Haven Court. As they approached the vicinity of their new house, the festive season was the most beautiful scenery with all the decorations on the houses and the garden nativity scene. They could see their Christmas tree from the distance, like a monument in the middle of the front lawn. There was an automatic remote built together with the gate and the garage. The tires just had to press into the sidewalk, and simultaneously, they would both open.

"This is pretty cool," said Peter. "I love it." One could see he was satisfied by just the way he smiled. For the first time, he was maneuvering all these alarms and codes by himself, which seemed quite understandable.

"Indeed, this is really a big house," Rose whispered. "It's a lot to get used to. We may have to get company, Peter."

"Like what company, Rose?"

"A dog and, of course, someone to help with the day-to-day cleaning and house cooking. We can't keep ordering in or eating out all the time. We would soon look like Humpty Dumpty," Rose said, laughing.

Peter was silent; he naturally did not see it funny.

The doorbell rang and scared both of them. "What's that?" Rose asked with a terrifying look.

It rang again. Peter spoke through the intercom. "Who is it?"

"It's delivery," the guy replied.

"Oh, okay, we'll be right there."

They both walked down the side path through the garden to another automatic gate, which only opened with Peter or Rose's thumbprints; that gate was used for deliveries only. The car was there with the dinner they ordered.

They began wondering how the driver figured out the entrance for delivery, not knowing that the Collinses ordered dinner from the same restaurant many times over the years and that the restaurant drivers were knowledgeable of the delivery entrance. Besides, there was a finger signpost pointing to that gate.

Dinner was great, but they hardly ate due to nervousness. They both needed to get themselves to consciousness that it was late and their wedding was only a few hours away.

Rose's cell phone rang, and the call showed her "Restricted." She showed the phone to Peter and asked him, "Should I answer? I'm not aware who could be calling me from a restricted number. If and when an unknown number calls me, it's usually one of the telemarketers."

Peter expressed that she should answer. "You never can tell," he said. "With tomorrow being the wedding day, someone from the guest list may need some sort of information."

"Hello, how may I help you?" Rose asked. "There is someone on the line, Peter, but they refuse to speak."

"Hello," Rose continued. "I know you are there. I'm waiting."

The party at the other end spoke two words. "He's mine." Then they hung up.

Rose was speechless; she dropped the phone and looked as if she was about to have a heart attack.

"What is the problem, Rose? What is it? Who was on the phone?"

Rose was stunned and livid at the same time. A plethora of emotions raced through her body; she could not respond to Peter. She was hurting and seriously confused because she recognized the voice to be that of Grace Milford. On the night she broke into Peter's house and created havoc, those were the same words she used then.

"I recognized that voice, Peter. It's Grace." Rose looked at Peter with disgust. "It's that woman again. How did she get my number? And why is she calling me? I thought she was incarcerated for a long time. Why is she always coming back? What is she expecting to get from us, Peter? Are you seeing her?"

"Oh, for Christ's sake, Rose, don't be stupid. How could I be seeing her? You and I have been together twenty-four-seven. How would this affair play out? Oh, Rose, not tonight. Tomorrow is our wedding day, and none of us have time for foolishness. I have not the foggiest idea why she called. She probably got your number from the wedding invitation the florist posted on Facebook or in the store, Rose."

"But she could not be in the store. She was sentenced to prison for a long time. I really don't understand, Peter. What's going on?" Rose began crying when Peter reached to comfort her. "Don't touch me, please. Do not touch me. There may not be a wedding tomorrow, Peter. I refuse to be married to you with Grace Milford being a monkey on my back, showing up as often as she does."

"Rose, why don't you stop?" Peter started yelling, his voice screeching with anger. "I have no idea why Grace called. She is supposed to be in prison. Let me call Sheriff Wakefield. He may be able to shed some light on this whole mystification. I won't even try to solve any of it myself. At this point, it's not fair to either of us to focus on this baloney."

Right away, Peter called the sheriff, who answered with a sleepy tone. Peter identified himself, and yes, he remembered who he was. "I know it's late, but I have a problem. I am not sure if you will be able to help."

"What is it, Peter?"

"Do you remember Grace Milford, the girl who tried twice to latch herself on to me?"

"Say no more," Sheriff Wakefield answered. "I do remember her. She is in prison, Peter, and will be there for a long time."

"Well, she just called my fiancée. First, she kept silent. Then all she said was 'He is mine,' the same words she used at my house at Matt Court when she broke in."

"Let me call the prison, Peter. I will call you right back. Don't worry, she had to be there."

In about half an hour, Sheriff Wakefield called. "Mr. Swazi, she probably called from prison. She is still there. She is only trying to aggravate your fiancée and bring confusion. Somehow, she found out you will be getting married tomorrow and maliciously thought of doing this. Don't worry, Peter, you are safe. Congratulations, happy holidays, and all the best for tomorrow's matrimony."

By this time, Rose showered, went to bed, and locked the bedroom door. When Peter was through talking with the sheriff, he called out for Rose. She locked herself in the bedroom and refused to answer or even open the door. "Rose, please do not play games tonight. I am asking you to open the door, please," Peter pleaded. "I need to talk with you. I would hate to have to break this door to come in, but if I have to, I will, so you might as well open it."

All the doors were remotely operated from the inside. If Peter had to break the door, that would set the alarm off secretly, and the police would have been there in seconds. Rose knew this; therefore, she opened the door.

"Why are you acting like this, Rose? It has to be a direct plan coming from the adversary."

"Why would this sort of hell break loose on a night like this?"

"You mean the night before our wedding? I refuse to have this. Sheriff Wakefield assured me by making a call to the prison, inquiring of her whereabouts, that she was still there and would be for years to come. He further mentioned she is doing this to frustrate us so that we get on each other's nerves. Sure enough, the wedding would be affected, one way or the other, or she is hoping there might not be one.

"I love you, Rose. I would never ever do anything like this to jeopardize our relationship or to engage in any wrongdoing against God and against the woman God gave me. I can understand your feelings, but you have to trust me. In any relationship, if trust is not there, a downfall is inevitable. We might as well cancel the wedding. It's not healthy for a woman to marry a man whom she does not trust. So what do we do, Rose? It's easier not to have a wedding than to go through a divorce. This is exactly what Grace wants. The saying goes, 'The fox could not get to the grapes. Therefore, he said they are sour anyway.' We need to rest, Rose, but I would like to know before I retire for the night. Are we getting married tomorrow? Or are we canceling the wedding? I would have to make calls tonight, mainly to Father Hurling."

What Peter hadn't noticed was Rose had fallen asleep while he babbled and did not hear most of his monologue.

Kneeling by the bed, Peter began praying, "Dear heavenly Father, we have foolishly reacted to a situation that makes no sense whatsoever. We realize this is the plan of the adversary and not the plan you promised us. We have seen your will for us in so many different ways. So, Lord, why is there uncertainty now? I don't believe you've brought us this far to leave us. Forgive us where we have doubted you. Forgive us for believing that the enemy has the power to ruin what you have created. In Jesus's name, amen."

At the end of Peter's prayer, Rose was awakened and was also in total agreement with an amen. She sat up on the side of the bed, with Peter still kneeling in front of her. They embraced each other for a long time through many tears and promised this would never happen again.

The bridal party arrived two hours before. Rose showed them to their separate dressing rooms. She had hired two ladies-in-waiting to make sure they were all in sync, especially with their attire, and to keep a check on their timing. The limousines were arranged to collect them for the church at twelve o'clock. The distance to Saint Paul's Cathedral took a half hour, but with the holiday traffic, delays were inevitable.

As the bridal party exited the front door, they were met by three photographers, snapping pictures of their every move. They were asked to walk across the well-manicured lawn with the picturesque, decked-out Christmas tree as the backdrop as they entered the black limousines.

The neighbors gathered just in time to see the bride enter her horse-drawn carriage with two white horses, accompanied by an entourage of police officers riding bikes just to make sure they were not delayed by traffic. Rose waved to every person on her way; she wore a beautiful organza, satin, and French lace dress with a fitted, off-the-shoulder bodice and puffy Cinderella bottom with a matching six-foot-long rhinestone-studded train. It was a beyond gorgeous wedding dress designed by Vera Wang, carried by David's Bridal.

Here came the horse-drawn carriage where Rose was seated, waving to the last of the crowd before she got ready to step down onto the roadway. The moment the bridal party entered Saint Paul's Court, there were onlookers lining both sides of the churchyard as if this was preplanned, waving and cheering as they arrived. They were ten minutes ahead of schedule, which Father Hurling liked very much; he had enough time to settle himself before the grand entry.

Her dream had finally become a reality. One year ago, Rose Alexander visited Saint Paul's Cathedral; at the time, she was on a sightseeing tour, envisioning that one day she would walk down that beautiful aisle to say "I do" at the altar to the man of her dreams. Today, December 24, Father Hurling—who had been the pastor of Peter's Mom for many years and who had always been praying for him, making sure he was okay—was proud to ask everyone to stand as the door reopened. Rose stood looking down the long aisle of Saint Paul's Cathedral with tears streaming down her cheek, tears of joy and laughter as destiny was fulfilled.

Father Hurling was already standing in front of the podium and signaled the church's musician to play a musical prelude for the bridal party as they entered. Everyone was asked to stand as they marched down the center aisle. It was such a solemn occasion. Guests were dabbing at their eyes; they were unable to hold back the tears as the organist played "Here Comes the Bride."

Ben Scott, her giveaway father, held her firmly, making sure her nervousness did not appear too noticeable. She hooked her arm in the crook of Ben's left elbow, and he placed the cup of his right hand over hers. And they slowly walked down the long aisle amid all the oohs, aahs, and gasps.

The ceremony began. Someone read from the Bible, "'Charity suffereth long, and is kind; charity envieth not; charity vaunteth not itself, is not puffed up, doth not behave itself unseemly, seeketh not her own, is not easily provoked, thinketh no evil'" (1 Corinthians 13:4–5, KJV).

Father Hurling prayed and then continued the wedding vows. He asked them to repeat after him: "I take you, Rose, to have and to hold from this day forward, for better or worse, for richer or poorer, in sickness and in health, to love and to cherish, until we are parted by death." Peter repeated the same vows, and they both solemnly affirmed.

The giving and receiving of rings was awesome. Father Hurling explained the significance of the rings being round—that love has no beginning and no ending—and prayed that their lives would be an exemplary one. They were pronounced husband and wife. Mr. and Mrs. Peter Swazi kissed and were then presented to the congregation.

There was Aunt Stella smiling at them while they were leaving for a photo session. With excitement, Rose rushed over and hugged her, thanking her for coming. "We'll see you at the reception, Aunt Stella." She was accompanied by her nurse and was only allowed two days to attend the wedding. It was a surprise to see her.

There were a lot of people on the outside, ready with cameras, taking pictures, blowing bubbles, and throwing petals. Among them was Rose's neighbor from New York, Mrs. Fields. "Oh my goodness, you have all decided to give me a real surprise." Rose's attorneys, David Klaus and Charles Glasgow, were also present. They chatted briefly as the photographers took them to a quiet area on the church's lawn, where they were photographed lengthily.

The Cliff called Peter, reminding him of the time to get there. They rode in a limousine instead of the carriage as time was of the essence. There was an entourage of cars crowding the parking lot of The Cliff. The limousine rolled into the reserved parking at the entrance to The Cliff's banquet hall.

It was amazing to see everyone there; it seemed there was no one missing from the invitation list. There weren't any cards left on the guest list table. The master of ceremonies asked everyone to stand as the bridal party entered, followed by the introduction of the newlyweds, Mr. and Mrs. Peter Swazi. There was thunderous applause as they walked to their beautifully decorated table. The Cliff did such a great job with the decor presentation; it was obvious they outdid themselves.

For the caliber of guests, Peter and Rose were awfully proud; they were satisfied with everything. They did their first dance, and at the end, quite a number of people were asked to offer a toast to each member of the bridal party. After dinner, the couple was delighted to move about, greeting and thanking everyone for coming. Peter gave his vote of thanks and shared how they met. It was a bit sad in a way, but he felt he had to.

"We have had quite a journey, even a near-death experience, just a few days before our wedding, but God kept us as He promised.

My wife lost her parents at a very young age, but I must thank them for having such a beautiful human being. I thank Aunt Stella, who stepped in and took the best care of raising her to be who she is. Aunt Stella, please stand."

She stood proudly and gave a royal wave. Everyone applauded.

Peter continued, "I lost my mother some months ago in that terrible storm. Since then, Rose has been more than a tower of strength. We became inseparable. In the midst of our friendship, I became aware that we were destined for each other."

"I thank everyone for taking the time from your busy schedule to be here. This speaks volumes. Without you, our wedding would not have been the success that it is. Special thanks to The Cliff, the manager and staff, who made this possible. We are so very grateful. We thank Ben Scott and his family, Abigail Suarez and her husband, and my best friend and ex-boss Richard Azan and his family. Thanks to Father Hurling and the friends of Saint Paul's Cathedral. You have been a tower of strength to us. Thanks so much."

Chapter 14

"The road we walked may have been a treacherous one. The hurdles we've crossed send us crashing into each other. The valleys we have gone through may have been dark, but we had someone who led us through to the light. Out of evil came the good. On behalf of my precious wife, compliments of the season. Please enjoy the holidays. Thank you."

It was an enjoyable wedding reception. The music began, and everyone started dancing.

Peter, with his bride, sneaked out the side exit door into a waiting limousine, which took them home. They were scheduled to depart on Christmas night for their honeymoon in Dubai. The limousine turned the corner just in time to see Grace Milford dashing in an almost moving vehicle that disappeared in the distance.

Peter and Rose looked at each other and gasped. "Rose, we are not going to say one word about this maniac tonight. This is our day, and I refuse to allow unwelcome interference to ruin it. Right now, I refuse to give way to emotion." Peter chuckled. "We were taken to the church in a horse-drawn carriage. It's a good thing it's not the carriage that's taking us home, or else, we would have an awfully long ride."

They both laughed and then Rose took her shoes off to relieve her tired feet. It was a great conversation as they relaxed in each other's arms, almost falling asleep and enjoying the ride home. There was a small entourage of people waiting outside their home when they got there.

"Peter, why are there people here?"

"Oh, they are here to see us getting in and to wish us all the best on our honeymoon. These are our immediate neighbors. Although the house is alarmed, each one keeps an eye out when they know there isn't anyone home. At least so I was told by Tom Collins."

"How do they know we are going on a honeymoon?"

"Everyone knows after a wedding, there is a honeymoon. Therefore, their assumption isn't wrong."

They were met by their help, Kitty, at the side of the limousine with warm throws to cover them as they quickly made their way inside. The neighbors waved, threw kisses, and began to disperse slowly. "How sweet of them," Rose commented.

"It's good to have great neighbors. I am so appreciative of their kind gesture."

"Are you both having a nightcap?" Kitty asked.

"No, just water will do, Kitty."

"You know, we are traveling tomorrow afternoon. I think we will turn in for the night. Thank you."

"Merry Christmas. See you in the morning."

They made their way to the unused master bedroom. They slept satisfied and fulfilled in each other's arms, happy that they had chosen to wait. They were awoken by a Christmas carol. *"Hark! The herald angels sing, 'Glory to the newborn King! Peace on earth and mercy mild, God and sinners reconciled.'"*[8] It was a beautiful Christmas carol that led them to their morning devotional.

The scripture Peter read was from the book of Matthew 1:23 (KJV), "Behold, a virgin shall be with child, and shall bring forth a

---

8   Boney M. "Hark the Herald Angel Sing." *Christmas with Boney M.* (1984).

son, and they shall call His name Emmanuel, which being interpreted is, God with us." Their prayers were filled with thanksgiving and praise to the Almighty for all He had done, guiding and protecting them in all their plans from the time they met up to the time of marriage, and for His continued blessings as they went to Dubai.

The smell of coffee livened up their appetites and expectations and sent them running to the breakfast table even before they were called. Kitty made them a sumptuous, hearty Christmas morning breakfast for newlyweds consisting of a Spanish omelet, Canadian bacon, an assortment of pastries, fresh fruits, and cranberry juice, which was good to the last drop. They spent most of the morning putting together last-minute items in their suitcases and making sure they had everything.

The flight was on time. They were almost asleep when Rose realized the aircraft was pushing back. The pilot announced they were second in line for departure. They held hands and prayed again for a safe journey and that God would be their guide throughout their entire honeymoon. It was obvious they took quite a few naps during meal service. They'd missed quite a few.

"It's a long flight, Peter. I am beginning to feel famished," Rose said.

Peter pressed the stewardess's button to request meals for both of them. They were in each other's arms when a stewardess stretched across and disabled the call light. "May I help you?" she asked.

They both turned and asked what meals were available at this time. "Oh my God!" Peter and Rose grabbed onto each other in disbelief and stared at her. "Grace!" they exclaimed. They could not believe it was Grace Milford. "Grace... Grace Milford, you again?"

"Yes. How may I help you?"

ABOUT THE AUTHOR

Eleanor Marjorie Riley

It is indeed incredible that the tiny island of Jamaica has produced so many gifted and world-recognized people—artists, scholars, and athletes. Some claim that the gifts of the country's most well-known residents are due to the water, others the food; the success, for instance, of a Jamaican Olympian champion and world record holder athlete was attributed to Jamaica's Trelawny Yam. So many Jamaicans have excelled abroad, and their remarkable success should not be taken for granted, especially when one thinks of the tremendous sacrifices Jamaicans often endure to accomplish their goals. Jamaica has truly produced another daughter of greatness. The United States, and indeed the world, has been richer for her relationship with God and her relentless drive to reach others for the kingdom.

ELEANOR RILEY

The international gospel singer and recording artiste has the following recorded albums:

From the Setback

Christmas at Home with Eleanor

Flying Higher

Goodness and Mercy

From My Heart

Unchanged

Watch the Lamb

Be Happy

My Story

Taste the Victory

Arise

Lord, Please Calm the Storms in Me

She is also the author of the well-read book *Rungs on My Ladder*.

Printed in the USA
CPSIA information can be obtained
at www.ICGtesting.com
LVHW010737081223
765873LV00006B/72

9 798890 415608